Vampire Soul

A HEARTBLAZE NOVEL

BOOK ONE OF EMMA'S SAGA

·ᘜO◗(Ꮣ(·◑ ⊖◗(◐

SHAY ROBERTS

SNOWFIRE PRESS

VAMPIRE SOUL: A HEARTBLAZE® NOVEL

Published by:
Snowfire Press
114 W Magnolia St, Suite 400-152
Bellingham, WA 98225
Email: info@snowfirepress.com

Cover design by Ravven: http://www.ravven.com

ISBN: 978-1-946994-07-3 (paperback)
ISBN: 978-0-9967261-0-8 (eBook)

First edition

Please email typos@shayroberts.com if you discover an error or experience any readability issues with this book.

For bonus stories, updates, newsletter, and giveaways go to:
http://shayroberts.com/vsbonus

Dedicated to the intelligent, strong, and nurturing women in my life.

VAMPIRE SOUL: A HEARTBLAZE NOVEL

Ebony Snakes

EMMA RUE

Author's Note:
The following novel is told from the point of view of several characters, each with their own unique perspectives on the evolving plot. If you are unaccustomed to this style of storytelling, it can be a little challenging at first, but read on and the separate threads will all come together in a rewarding way.

TODAY IS THE BEST DAY of my whole pathetic life. Growing up in the foster care system, I never thought I'd get this far. But look at me now, first day of college, sitting in the front row, waiting for class to begin. I love starting over in a new place. Nobody here knows about my…special ability. No one is scared of me. No one hates me. Yet.

The professor, I think his name is Leeks, is late, and the students are grumbling. I hear he's a jerk, but he's the only one teaching *Europe to 1600* and I'm really excited about this material.

There's a preppy girl in a pink cashmere cardigan sitting next to me. She's smirking at my thrift store combat boots. She's wearing a gallon of vanilla perfume. What a subtle scent. She better not go near any open flames.

Some of us can't afford cashmere. Most days I wear a pair of black leggings and an oversized sweater. Preppy girl's pink leather shoe-boots probably cost more than my entire wardrobe.

Shouldn't snark. Today is a good day. Not just my first day of college, it's also my nineteenth birthday. I haven't told anyone, not even Melita, my mentor and best friend. I love her, but I'd really like to celebrate alone with a good book and some wine. I got a bottle from my apartment manager for babysitting a pair of polydactyl cats that vomited all weekend. Good times.

Still no sign of Professor Leeks. How long should we wait before giving up? I feel a jolt of anticipation as I remember that I'm meeting Micah after class. This will be my second self-defense lesson with him. Micah was worried when he found out I live in a bad neighborhood in East Providence. Before college, he was a soldier. He knows everything about fighting but doesn't brag about it. I have to pry everything out of him. He's ten years older than me, but I've thought about asking him out. He's incredibly good-looking, with dark hair and those sad blue eyes. But he's more than that; he's…enigmatic. Ooh, I love that word.

Micah is special. Maybe too special. Men like him notice

things. I need a man who won't notice things, who won't try to figure out my secret. But I can't stay away from Micah. I want him to run his fingers through my hair. I want him to whisper in my ear as he…

Professor Leeks suddenly enters the room, a whirlwind of tweed pretension. I immediately look past his face and into his soul, an ability I've had since childhood. Something is wrong. Very wrong. I stiffen in my seat.

I've seen his soul somewhere before. It looks like twisting ebony snakes. He's a bad man, an evil man, but I can't remember where I've seen that terrible soul.

As he approaches me with an armful of handouts, the back of my neck feels so cold that it burns. I'm overwhelmed with terror. I feel like he wants to kill me.

I leap from my seat and stumble over my backpack on the floor. He reaches toward me, and I use a fighting move that Micah taught me in our last session, a front kick. As my foot flies toward him, I know my life will never be the same again.

My boot smashes into his crotch. Leeks grunts and drops like a sack of rocks, handouts drifting down like snow. Only then do I realize that he wasn't reaching for me, he was reaching for my fallen backpack. Was he trying to help me?

Preppy girl shrieks. The whole class stares at me in stunned disbelief. They look like bystanders at a mugging; no one wants to be the first to intervene.

Professor Leeks sucks air like an emphysema patient as he struggles to his feet.

I don't understand what's happening, but I know I have to get out of here. I have to get somewhere safe. I grab my pack and flee the room like a criminal, followed by the gasps and whispers of the students.

What have I done? I've ruined my beautiful dream. Today is the worst day of my whole pathetic life. I wonder if I'll make it off campus before security gets the order to shoot the girl in the cheap combat boots.

Nesting Doll

STEFAN HILDEBRAND

WARRIORS DON'T THINK LIKE civilians. We don't have time to worry about stupid crap like what color of socks to wear today. I don't let my mind wander. Every second of the day is spent on threat assessment. I'm doing it now as I sit in this busy coffee shop, waiting for Emma Rue.

People come and go through the shop's squeaky glass door, most of them oblivious to their environment. If sidewalks ended in cliffs, half of Providence would be dead by tomorrow, their faces in their phones as they poured over the edge like lemmings. You need to look for the people who are actually paying attention. Watch the watchers, they told me in training, because some of them are paranormals. So I don't look into my drink as I sip it; I keep my eyes up, watching for the watchers.

I finish my coffee milk and push away the glass. They use actual glass here, not plastic. Coffee milk—cold milk blended with coffee syrup—must be a Rhode Island thing because there's nothing like it in my region of Vermont. It hurts to think about home. I gotta stop that. Maybe I'll have another coffee milk.

A blonde across the room looks over at me, a tilt to her head and a shy smile on her glossy lips. I get that a lot. Mom says I have my dad's devilish looks. Mom. I'm thinking of home again. Shit.

Where's Emma? We were going to walk over to the park so I could show her a technique. I can't believe she lives alone in such a bad neighborhood. I hope she's okay. I'd call, but she doesn't carry a phone. She's weird like that, but in a good way.

I was ordered to get close to Emma as part of my surveillance mission. She seems slow to trust people, and she should be. She thinks my name is Micah. I'm supposed to be a sophomore in some of her classes, but I'm almost ten years older. I told her I was in the army, coming late to college. But I didn't come for college, I came for her, and I'm not in any army she has ever heard of. The army I fight for is everywhere and nowhere, an army as old as the Roman Empire.

All this undercover work is wearing me down. I think of myself as one of those wooden dolls from Russia—you open it and there's another doll nesting inside, and then another. Where's the real me? I just keep getting smaller and smaller.

A thin dude with a sharp face steps into the coffee shop, his right hand stuffed into a pocket of his leather jacket.

His hidden hand clutches something. I glance at the table, real wood tattooed by a decade of coffee rings. Would it stop a bullet? I could use it as a shield while I rush him. His scrawny hand emerges, holding his wallet. Another threat averted. But I don't relax. Someday, some other dude will be coming for me. It's a miracle it hasn't happened already.

I can't wait around for Emma; I'll be late for the execution at Fort Adams. I was the junior member of the capture team. They'll be pissed if I miss it. They're using a soul cage. Never seen one in action. Never wanted to. My gut cramps at the thought of it.

As I rise from the table, I pluck an antacid from a roll in my shirt pocket. Wintergreen flavor. It takes a roll of these to get my stomach through the day.

Emma rushes through the door, looking upset, and hurries over to my table. "Micah, I'm so sorry. I had a problem at school."

I really have to go. But I find myself wanting to know about her problem. I gesture to the seat across from me. "I only have a minute."

We sit, and she twists her brown hair around one finger. "I think we should stop the self-defense lessons. But I hope we can still study together."

Something bad has happened. I see her hand trembling. "Why stop?"

She pauses, peering into my face like she's looking right through me. "Have you ever been tempted to … misuse … your fighting skills?"

"How do you mean?"

"I just used that move you taught me last time. On Professor Leeks."

"He attacked you?"

"No. That's the problem. He just got too close to me and I kicked him."

Wow. She doesn't seem like the kind of girl to freak out like that. It sounds like PTSD. Has she been assaulted in the past? What do I say to her? This kind of stuff is above my pay grade. "Sorry to hear that. Sounds like you could use someone to talk to. Maybe an expert?"

Tears glint in her violet eyes. "A counselor, a shrink?"

I'm making her cry. And that's bothering me. Not good. Where's my professional detachment? She's a surveillance target. This is just another job. I reach across the table and squeeze her hand. It feels warm, alive, charged with electricity. "I wish I could hang out but I have a thing."

Her pale face turns as hard as marble. "Go. I'm fine."

For some reason it's hard to let go of her hand. She isn't "fine" and neither am I. You know it's a shitty day when you have to abandon a crying girl to attend an execution. Part of me wants to stay, but there's nothing for it. As my dad likes to say, *hurry to act, worry distracts.* So I rise from the table. "Sorry, Emma. Let's talk more later."

She nods a goodbye as I leave the table, shoving another antacid into my mouth as I go. I'll need two rolls today.

Blue Dog

YOUNG EMMA RUE

THIRTEEN YEARS EARLIER

TODAY I AM SIX YEARS OLD. I want a cake, but they won't give me one because of the bad thing that happened last time.

Mr. Lindquist is digging in his shiny black briefcase where he keeps his secrets. Ms. Katy let him in her office to meet me again. I have to sit in the tall chair that makes my legs hurt. Last time I put gum under it when no one was looking.

I don't like Mr. Lindquist. He has small eyes and big glasses and his forehead sweats. He smiles, but when I look inside him I can see he is mad. He comes here every month and this month he wants to talk to me again. Maybe he will talk about my birthday.

He looks up from his secrets and sees me through his big glasses. "Hello, Maggie, where were we last?"

He doesn't know who I am! "I'm Emma Rue."

"Oh, yes, yes." He digs around in his briefcase. "Emma, yes, of course, I see."

"I'm six today." *There are six petals on Ms. Katy's desk flower and six spots on the wall behind Mr. Lindquist. I'm a good counter.*

"Katy Sydow wanted me to speak with you about these *things* you've been seeing."

"Ms. Katy said I wouldn't get in trouble for telling."

I lean forward and reach for a book in his briefcase but he pulls it back. I like books. You can make them stop when you want. I wish I could make people stop. His book is purple and green. I bet it's a good book.

"You're not in trouble, Emma, but some of the things you've said have upset the other children in your group home. I need to understand why you said them." He is smiling but inside he is trying to trick me.

I shouldn't talk now. *Shut up Emma.* I reach under the chair. The gum is hard now. It was peppermint and I liked it.

"You told Ms. Sydow that you can see what people are feeling inside. What did you mean by that?"

Shut up, Emma. Shut up, Emma. He moves in his chair and it sounds like a fart. I know it's bad to laugh now but I can't help it. He frowns and I stop laughing.

"Emma, it's important that you talk to me. We can clear this up and you can go play. But if you don't talk to me, you'll have to stay here while I bring in other people. Wouldn't you rather go play?"

I nod. I can hear the other kids playing outside, all of

us kids who can't get foster parents. None of them talks to me because I always know when they try to trick me. But I still want to go out on the slide. I'm the only one who's not afraid to go backward.

"Emma, what did you mean when you said you can see what people are feeling inside?"

I will tell him a little and he will let me go. "I look at your face. Then I look harder and I can see inside. There are lots of colors and they jump around."

"And these colors tell you what I am feeling?"

I nod. "I can see if you are happy or sad, if you are mean or nice."

He looks scared inside. I think I said the wrong answer.

Ms. Katy and Mr. Lindquist said I wouldn't get in trouble. Liars! They always say not to lie, but they lie more than us kids. Now I sit on my hard bed in the white jail, hugging Blue Dog. He is my best friend. My mother left him with me when she went away. I cried too much and his blue fur is all wet now.

The orderly is coming. I hear him stomping in the hall. I hate him. He has a mean face and he is even meaner inside.

I crawl under the hard bed and tell Blue Dog to be very quiet. There is a dust bunny under the bed. I see it move when the orderly opens the door. The bunny wants to run but there is no place to go.

I see the orderly's feet. He has black sneakers with black

laces. They look like evil feet.

His voice always sounds like he has a cold. "Emma, get out here right now!"

He knows I'm hiding! He will be mad if I stay here. I try to move but I can't. I'm shaking and my legs won't go.

The orderly reaches under the bed and grabs my foot. He pulls me out into the light like a monster who is eating me. I want to scream, but it makes him madder when I scream.

He takes Blue Dog away and leans close to whisper to me. "I'm getting tired of this, you little bitch."

I try not to cry but I can't help it. Blue Dog is my only friend. "Please give him back!"

"Here's the deal—you get him back when you stop causing trouble for me." He grabs Blue Dog's neck. "But any more shit like this, and I'll twist off his head. You understand me?" He turns Blue Dog's head around and I hear a tearing sound.

"Don't twist him! I'll be good."

"That's right you will!"

The orderly hurts my arm as he pulls me up and drags me out into the hall. It's hard to talk because I'm crying so much. "Where are you taking me?"

Through my blurry tears I see his mouth move. "You'll see."

Red Memories

EMMA RUE

THE PRESENT

It rolls across my palm, an inch-long capsule, half black and half white. My shrink wants me to swallow this skunk pill. He's hiding in his office while I sit in his tiny waiting room. I should have taken it five minutes ago, but something is stopping me. I keep thinking about that sadistic orderly in the pediatric psych ward who tormented me as a girl. After he filled me with needles, he would stuff a giant horse pill in my mouth and force it down with warm water. Ever since then I've had a hard time with pills.

A guppy in a nearby aquarium turns to face me, its mouth pulsing wide as if to say "take the pill." The tank smells like a wet dog, and the gurgling water makes me want to pee. I feel a tug on my scalp and realize I'm doing it again, wrapping my hair around my finger. We all have our odd habits, but mine are especially odd or they wouldn't be feeding me crazy pills.

It seems that kicking your professor in the balls is frowned upon. I've been temporarily suspended and they sent me to this shrink downtown. I still have no idea why I did it. Part of me desperately wants to know and part of me is afraid to know.

I've seen a hundred counselors, psychologists, and shrinks over the years, but this is the first one who wants to do a drug-induced hypnotic regression. He wants me to remember details about my childhood. Such lovely times! My mother abandoned me as an infant and everything went downhill from there.

These are not things I want to remember, and I don't know if I can trust this doctor. I remember his face when he tilted the paper cup and the skunk pill landed heavy in my hand. Beneath his smile, there was something complex, a strange kaleidoscope of guilt, shame, and excitement. I suspect this is an experimental regression drug and I am his lab rat.

I jump as the air conditioning kicks in with a rattle. Why did that startle me? The air is frigid but I realize I'm covered with sweat. This pill scares me. My instincts whisper *run*. But if I don't finish this therapy, the college will kick me out for good. I love studying history, and I don't want to lose my chance for an education.

My shrink's little voice drifts out of his office. He is not a little man but he has a little voice. "Emma, how's it going out there?" He's eager to begin his experiment.

Oh, what the hell. Even if there's only a small chance

that hypnosis will help me understand myself, it's worth the risk. I shove the pill in my mouth and follow it with a gulp of water. I can feel it burrowing its way down to my stomach.

∞♡∞

The shrink tells me to imagine I'm in a 'happy place'. Wow, I have sooo many to choose from! I've decided it's the history section of the Athenaeum, where I work part-time in the evenings. When I was in high school, I took AS220 classes on papermaking and book arts. Digital books are great, but paper books are living history, especially the rare books. I love to check the publication dates. Sometimes, if I stare long and hard at an old book, I see faint swirls of color, as if I am looking into the soul of a person. Old books are alive, in their own way.

I'm lying on my shrink's sofa, trying to cooperate with the regression, but he's not making it easy. Two ginger mints bounce around in his mouth like a pair of bones in a bag. He needs four mints to hide that breath. I will tell him anything about my childhood if he stops breathing in my direction.

The pill suddenly has me feeling warm and tingly, as if I could dream without being asleep. Maybe I'm wrong about this drug. It feels fantastic. Something like this would make sex with Micah wicked fun. Micah? We've never had sex. Have we? No. Other boys, but not Micah. Maybe we'll go back to his place after my self-defense lesson.

My mind begins to drift and I feel Micah standing behind me, his hands on my hips. He's been saying something about my center of gravity but I haven't been listening. How can he act so casual when he's touching me? Doesn't he know how it makes me feel? Every girl in the park can see it on my face. Even smart boys can be stupid sometimes.

Micah whispers into my ear, "Lift your knee first, then kick. Strike with the ball of your foot."

I kick awkwardly, purposely losing my balance and falling into his arms.

His voice grows more businesslike. "Emma, you are now resting comfortably in a peaceful state of relaxation. You are safe and secure here. Nothing you remember can hurt you."

I'm confused. I thought we were at the park, but now Micah is sitting beside me with a schoolbook under one arm. Oh, that's right, I canceled our lessons. That's okay. Micah was a soldier. He'll protect me. I am safe with him.

Is he mad at me for bailing on him? "Micah, I'm sorry I canceled. Learning moah about fighting ... dammit, *more*." Despite my best efforts to lose my Rhode Island accent, I still sometimes drop the "r" on certain words, especially when I'm tired or drunk.

Micah puts his hand on the back of mine. Somehow it doesn't feel right. "Emma, we're here to remember. I want you to think back to when you were ten years old. Do you remember being ten?"

I nod, or I think I do. I can't feel my head.

"Who was your favorite person when you were ten?"

I remember Will's salt-and-pepper beard. "He brings me cheese sandwiches from home."

"Who brings you sandwiches, Emma?"

"Will, the janitor at Saint Mary's."

"Good, Emma. You are doing great. You are at peace, safe and secure."

"I'm hungry."

"You can eat soon, but first I'd like you to go back further, to when you were five. Do you remember being five?"

Yes. There are five candles on my cake with white frosting.

"Emma?"

"Five candles."

"Who was your favorite person when you were five?"

Ms. Hampton is talking on the phone in the other room. She talks and talks for hours, but never to me. I hold my finger over a candle until my skin turns red. I want to scream from the pain, but Ms. Hampton will come back, and I want to be alone with Blue Dog and my cake.

"Emma, who is your favorite person?"

"Blue Dog. He barks a sound that only dogs can hear. I'm saving a piece of cake for him." I set Blue Dog next to the cake. He wants to lick the frosting, but he has no tongue. He is muddy from when I took him outside. "I'm hungry. Don't get mud on my cake!"

"Emma, you are at peace, safe and secure. Now I want

you to go even further back. To a time *before* you were a baby, before you were Emma."

Before? What was before? I sense there is something from before. But it scares me. "There's nothing from before."

"Now Emma, it's very important that you concentrate. These are only memories. They can't hurt you."

They will hurt me. I know this. "There's nothing."

Micah's voice hardens. "Emma, you're an adult now, and adults sometimes have to do difficult things. So answer my question. Do you remember a time before you were a baby, a time from a past life?"

A memory creeps toward me like a demon in the dark.

Low fog shrouds a harbor dimly lit by a crescent moon. The limp sail of a corsair hovers above the white blanket like a decapitated head. I smell rum and body odor. Through the mist I see the twisting colors of a sailor's vile soul. He lies passed out drunk on a damp wooden dock. How convenient.

"Emma? Are you remembering?"

"I'm hungry." I glide to the sailor in silence and crouch like a lioness over her prey. My blonde hair sweeps his face as I sniff his neck. His blood smells like vinegar, but I am famished. I feel my thorns extend against my will. Perhaps just a taste.

I pin him to the dock with my white-gloved hands and nuzzle his neck. I tingle with anticipation as his blood finds my tongue. He tastes like worm-riddled hardtack soaked in urine. I withdraw quickly, clumsily, tearing his flesh. His eyes flutter open as twin streams of blood spurt from his neck. The foul liquid finds the gap in my black woolen cape and stains my periwinkle bodice.

"Emma, who is your favorite person in this memory?"

Julian is my favorite person. The love of my life. I wore this dress for Julian. And now it's ruined. The sailor sees his blood and screams. I grab his hair and knock his head against the dock. Too hard. His skull makes a wet thump against the rough wood. Oh dear, it seems I've killed him.

"No!" I hear myself crying as I clamber to my feet. I'm back in the office now.

Micah stares at me calmly, but on the inside he's as scared as me. "Emma, tell me what you remember."

"Bad dream. Blood." I fall into his arms. "I was killing someone."

My tears drip onto Micah's shoulder. I am so weak, so stupid. Tears are for little girls. Maybe it's the pill he gave me. It's messing with my brain. I shouldn't have taken that pill from him. Him. Him. My shrink! I thought my shrink was Micah! A wave of nausea hits me as I push him away. Up close, I can see the red vessels in the whites of his narrow eyes. "What was in that pill?"

"I told you, Emma, it's a memory enhancer. It's designed to facilitate the regression."

I look into his face. Calm on the outside but excited underneath. "We were supposed to talk about my childhood, not what came before."

"We were supposed to find the trauma that has been contributing to your poor decision-making, and we're making amazing progress!" He grins.

I want to punch him in his stupid smiling face. But instead, I head for the office door.

"Emma, I'm afraid you need to stay."

His odd tone gives me goose bumps. I pause at the door.

"You have a special sort of problem that requires a special sort of treatment. We need to get you the proper help."

Run, says a voice inside me. Still wobbly from the drug, I stumble out of the office and into the waiting room. I feel his hands on me and jerk away. Suddenly, I'm falling. I reach out and grab the aquarium. It slides behind the table at an angle, sloshing water on me. As I sit up on the floor, the guppy flops in my lap, mouth pulsing wide in silent screams. I scoop it up and return it to what's left of the water.

My shrink is on the phone, speaking fast and low. "I've confirmed your suspicions."

Who is he talking to? Not the police. I grab my pack and rush for the exit. Why isn't he blocking the way? A sudden fear stabs me. What if the door is locked?

Witch Tree

CYNTHIA GREENE

Being a ghost has its perks. Bill's pathetic wife has no idea that I am in her head, seeing through her eyes. Bill lies stretched out on Egyptian cotton sheets in a beautiful hotel room, glistening in the afterglow. He's lost none of his manly charms.

It's been nearly two decades since we were engaged. Two decades since he left me heartbroken after his malicious family convinced him that "poor Cynthia" was insane.

It should be *me* sharing his bed, not this heifer he calls a wife. She rolls her nude and sweaty body away from him, and now I'm stuck staring at the ceiling. Bessie, be a good cow and roll back over where I can enjoy the view. She obviously needs some encouragement, so I fill her eyes with the image of a spider on the ceiling. She hates spiders.

I can't read her mind, but I can sense her fear. It feels exhilarating. She clutches at Bill, looking for comfort in his soft brown eyes, sprinkled with flecks of gold. There was a time when he could not tear those eyes from my face. I would weep for those days if only I had eyes to weep. At least I can watch these weekly motel matinees, Bill's futile attempt to sustain his sex life away from a house with young twins.

Far from here, I sense someone approaching my final resting place. The groundskeeper? I should investigate. Sadly, it seems that my special time with Bill is over.

A group of drug-addled teens crowds around my modest grave at Highland Memorial in Johnston. I'm now seeing through the eyes of some counterculture girl. Bite marks chip her black fingernails. She takes a long puff from a marijuana cigarette. *That's bad for your ovaries, you ignorant child. You'll never have babies that way.* Kids today don't take care of their bodies. I blame the parents. The judge asked why I killed the mothers of those neglected children. This is why. Bad parents are worse than no parents. They create little monsters.

An unkempt boy sidles up to my headstone. He draws down the zipper of his sagging pants and they all bray like donkeys as he urinates on my headstone. Where is that worthless groundskeeper? I'm so angry I could scratch out this delinquent's eyes!

My mind leaps across the space from the smoking girl to the peeing boy. During the jump, I see nothing but darkness. A woman needs eyes to see. I had eyes once, as gray as polished steel. But I lost them when I hanged myself to escape that horrible prison. I expected to reach heaven. But instead, I found myself on earth, living as a ghost. I would have preferred to go to hell.

As the urinating boy begins to zip up, I enter his head. He looks down and I make him see a writhing black snake with yellow eyes jutting from his pants. He yelps and scrambles backward, falling hard on his backside. He swats at his groin, trying to brush the snake away, and screams at the self-inflicted pain. The donkeys bray. If this goes well, he will tear off his own genitals. I'm so very pleased with my little trick!

Suddenly, darkness falls and I'm spiraling toward the witch tree. Even without eyes, I can see Rowan's magic sigil, with its spider-leg branches and serpentine roots. She summons me, her ghostly servant, no doubt to torment one of her enemies. I feel a jolt of fear. Facing this ancient witch, perhaps the most powerful being in this world and the next, always unnerves me. What will happen if I fail this frightening woman, a creature whose cruelty knows no limits?

❧♡❧

With no body of my own to inhabit, Rowan lends me hers. I see through her eyes as she sits before a candlelit mirror with a gilded frame, but I can't make out the details of the shadowy room behind her.

I've never seen Rowan's face. She always wears a mask of

twisted leaves that makes her look like some sort of goblin. Her emerald eyes pierce the mask, cold and hard, watching me watching her.

"I have a task for you, Cynthia Greene." Her singsong voice has an Irish accent.

She always addresses me by my full name. I've no idea why. I wish she would send me back so I could conclude my business with the urinating boy. But I dare not ask. I use her body to speak; her mask moves ever so slightly as her mouth forms my words. "Yes, Mistress, I'm eager to perform your task."

"Well and good then. I'm sending you on a hunt. If you succeed, a wondrous reward will be yours. But fail me, and you'll find yourself lost in the metaverge, drifting in an eternity of darkness." Her final sentence echoes like rolling thunder but does little to dampen my sudden hope.

What reward? Dare I ask? I must. "A body, Mistress? Will that be my reward?"

Rowan's goblin mask tilts in a shallow nod.

Finally, a body, after a whole year without one! Let it be a young and beautiful body! I could return to a career at Child Protective Services. I could seduce Bill away from his wife. I could at long last have children. I shall be an excellent mother! I speak quickly through Rowan's lips. "I will do whatever you ask, Mistress."

Rowan leans toward the mirror, close enough for her breath to cloud it. Candlelight dances on the silver threads of her forest-green gown. Her voice drops to a whisper. I have never heard her whisper. "Your quarry is a girl named Emma Rue."

Boxing Day

STEFAN HILDEBRAND

TRAFFIC WAS BAD. From my meeting with Emma, it took an hour to get to Fort Adams. I'll probably miss the execution. I'm fine with that. Killing someone in combat is one thing, but watching a civilian scream as they box him up is not my idea of a good time.

I park my car in the lot outside the fort and watch the sun set over Newport Harbor. A warm spring wind pushes a dozen sailboats across Narragansett Bay. I like the smell of saltwater. It clears my head and helps me focus.

The fort is managed by a trust. But few people know the trust is controlled by the Knights of Rome. Publicly, the trust is all about preserving our national heritage, but its real purpose is to preserve our *human* heritage. KoR hunts and kills the paranormals that most people think are just stories and myths. They have been doing it, and doing it well, since the reign of Roman emperor Constantine the Great. KoR recruited me as a teenager, after I won a regional Taekwondo tournament. All they saw was a promising martial artist, someone they could mold. They were blind to the real me.

I pass through security at the north gate. It's a busy day. Fifty or sixty tourists roam the parade grounds. Fort Adams is one of Newport's historic attractions. The Knights of Rome hide in plain sight.

I step into a concave gun emplacement lined with stone. It's empty now, but at the time of the Civil War, a Rodman cannon perched here. It could fire a 300-pound projectile over three miles. This fort had the reach to control the entire bay area.

I pass by the gun emplacement's rusty iron mounting rod. It's actually a sensor that identifies me. Then I walk under a crumbling brick arch, through a debris-filled corridor, and down hidden stone stairs leading to a secret door disguised as a dead end. At this moment, the door will open to my touch and no other.

I've used this entrance a lot. But today it looks somehow … threatening. I become aware that my fingers are "talking" again, a type of nervous, random sign language. Shit, I'm a wreck. I chew another antacid and head through the door.

Under the fort are a series of sleek floors, each a different color. Stony-eyed guards with silverweave body armor and assault rifles monitor everyone. I go through security at Level Blue and take the elevator down to Level Red.

I walk slowly, in no hurry to see an execution that is probably already over. I don't really need to, but I turn to pass through the ludus to check on the intermediate dagger class. The smell of sweat and adrenaline hits me before I get there. It's not as good as saltwater, but almost.

Marco is teaching tonight. As usual, his black sweats are dry and seemingly starched.

The class catches sight of me and stops, nodding their respect. It still feels weird. Half of them are older than me; most have been knighted. Yet I'm the one being groomed for Artufex. Marco bows but his eyes never leave me. I taught him that.

The execution chamber sits at the end of the longest hall on Level Red, a long walk for the condemned. I step into the tiny chamber. There's barely room for four people on the safe side of the unbreakable glass barrier.

The observers are here. Damn, the execution hasn't happened yet. Fortunata Golde, a bitch forged in iron and quenched in piss, flashes me a sour look. Getting knighted didn't mellow her, it just made her angrier. I'm her inferior, unknighted, still in training, yet somehow squired to Henry Cobo, the greatest Artufex who ever lived; I may even take his place. And Fortunata's not okay with that.

She can fight better than me but her surly attitude doesn't work with the students. Marco may be dead inside but at least he wants to see you improve. Fortunata wants to see you fail. That isn't the KoR way, so now she's heading up a field ops unit, the unit that failed to catch the vampire they're boxing today. It was *my* training unit that brought him in. Fortunata's probably gonna kill me one day. I hope they don't believe the suicide note.

My stomach's aching but I won't pop antacids in front of the observation group. Beyond this dimly lit room, on the other side of the window, rests a soul cage on a low stone table. Open and empty, the chrome coffin reflects the light of the small candles around the table. But it's not really chrome, of course; it's a composite metal called *plaga*.

In the old days, paranormals were burned, but that wasn't very smart. Sometimes they came back in a future life to wreak havoc. So the Knights of Rome developed plaga, a special metal that prevents the soul from escaping. When the prisoner dies inside the plaga coffin, their soul remains trapped inside with their body. Then the coffin is lowered into a deep underground vault used for radioactive waste so strong it will fry anyone who approaches.

A technician in a black hood checks the lethal gas canisters inside this shiny new coffin. Any moment they'll bring out the prisoner, a chunky boy in his late teens who thought it would be fun to be a real vampire. Right now he's probably puking up his guts. They have a special bucket for that. I've seen it.

Light floods the observation room as one of the office runners, a guy with the complexion of a minefield, rushes in and whispers to me in a girlish voice. "They want you on Level Black. The Hall of Regents." His eyes shine with awe.

My stomach does a flip. Somehow I'd rather watch the execution than go to the Hall of Regents.

I've been to Level Black only once before. They took me to the Hall of Records to take my vows. I can still remember those simple words...

I pledge my loyalty to the Knights of Rome. I pledge to fight the enemies of mankind with all my strength and valor. I pledge to put faith before fear and group before glory. If I should break these vows, I shall forfeit my eternal soul. So swear I, Stefan Hildebrand.

I step off the elevator and enter the eerily dark halls of Level Black. On the wall across from the elevator hangs the Knights of Rome emblem, a gold laurel wreath on a crimson background. The wreath curves like the wings of a predatory bird.

There are no guards here. None of them has the clearance. I doubt they need guards anyway. I'm sure if I set foot in here without permission I'd somehow explode on the spot.

An old, grim-faced man approaches. I've got no idea who he is. He grabs my shoulder without a word and leads me through a labyrinth of hallways that all look alike. Most people couldn't make it back without help. I think he's circling to confuse me.

We finally stop, and the grim man's bony hand turns me toward a pair of bronze-clad doors that show a relief of a Roman battle. He speaks in a whisper. "Hall of Regents. Don't knock—they'll open it when they're ready."

The black halls swallow the man as he retreats. I stand alone before the bronze doors.

What do the Regents want? From the stories I've heard, only epic events happen here, most of them bad.

Suddenly, I know why I'm here. They've discovered my secret, what I've been hiding for years. I've been careful not to make any close friends here, anyone who could rat me out. But I slipped up somehow. I guess it was only a matter of time.

A mechanism grinds and the doors crack open.

I stumble back. The hallway spins. My fingers cramp as they dance about in their insane sign language. When I'm really stressed, they have a mind of their own.

The heavy doors swing wide open, inviting me to my doom. I can smell something sweet.

BLAHBLAHTINE

EMMA RUE

As I APPROACH my apartment building, I expect men in white coats to pounce on me and drag me back to the shrink I escaped, but no one is here. My eyes flit nervously across a lovely "yard" made of dirt and litter and past the building's front door, hanging on one hinge. Maybe someone's waiting for me inside.

I walk carefully into the lobby and retrieve my mail from a row of graffiti-covered boxes. The paint is still wet on a new, unreadable missive.

Once inside my apartment I begin to relax a little. My living room is small and cluttered, just how I like it. I've been told that's a symptom of depression, along with my social isolation. Maybe so, but I've never seen this place as a home, just a place to sleep. In this neighborhood, the rental applications are short and no one cares if you've had an eviction. I've had some problems in the past. No one ever taught me how to manage money. I toss my mail and my keys down next to a beige sofa that I salvaged from the curb. The fabric is stained but it was free so I make do. Some nights I fall asleep there with a book in my hand.

The musky smell of drying paper reminds me to check on my project in the kitchen. At Saint Mary's they made me keep a therapy journal. Over 200 handwritten pages. I'm recycling it to make new paper, mixing shredded purple petals into the pulp. I've liked violets ever since Billy Morton told me they were the same color as my eyes, just before he put his hand under my dress. He pulled back a nub.

I check my mobile phone for messages. Instead of keeping it on me, I always leave it in my apartment. Gadgets break if I'm near them for too long. People say it's just bad luck, but it's something more. I know this. I discover that my shrink has left a message apologizing for the "reaction" I had to the medication. He wants to schedule a follow-up appointment. Why yes, I'd love another opportunity to achieve personal enlightenment in your chamber of horrors. Thank you for asking!

I return to the living room. It's really more of a book room. I have no computer or television. The walls are covered with bookshelves I've made from planks and cinder blocks scavenged from my disintegrating neighborhood. Used books are nearly free if you know where to find them; I currently own 1,347. Most of them are history books. I especially like biographies: John Adams, Mary Wollstonecraft, George III, and Thomas Jefferson. The figures of the late eighteenth century seem especially real to me.

I plop down on my street sofa and look at the mail. There's a flyer for pizza I can't afford, even with the coupon. And carpet cleaning? I think not. There are creatures in my carpet that date back to the Cretaceous period. Disturb them at your own risk.

At the bottom of the mail pile is a letter from the school.

I've been expelled! Months ago, I put some "creative information" on my scholarship application. It was the only way I had a prayer of getting in. Now they've found out and I'm busted. I should have realized the bastards would give me a closer look after I kicked Leeks. What irony, I won the scholarship but now I don't need it.

What am I going to do? I love school. I was going to get my doctorate and teach at a university while I wrote books. The first one was going to be about George III. I'm convinced that he wasn't insane but was actually poisoned, and I want to go to England to find the source material to make my case.

Now I'll have to find another college. Will they make me start over? Will they even accept me after what I've done?

I suddenly realize there's another repercussion. Some of that scholarship money is paying my rent! My work at the Athenaeum is only part-time, so I've got to find a second job, and right now, or I'll be homeless. I have no relatives I can live with. There's only Melita, the closest thing I have to a mom. Melita looks out for me. She was my mentor in the Big Sisters program. She works in circulation at the Athenaeum and got me a job there, which would have been impossible without her help. Melita is raising two kids in a small apartment so there's really no room for me at her place. She can't know about this; she would want to give me her bed while she slept on the floor.

Tears fill my eyes and I reach for…

What the hell was that? For a moment, I was reaching for someone, looking for comfort. I'm alone here, yet I have the strangest feeling that I live here with someone.

Julian?

No, I live alone. Julian is the man I was dreaming about in the shrink's office. Or was it just a dream? What if it was a real memory from a past life? Or maybe the shrink used the drug to put these ideas in my head. What if he's trying to brainwash me somehow? Maybe, but I doubt it. I've always been weird in the head. And I'm physically different as well, making gadgets break around me. Melita says I have a *magnetic personality.*

If this was an actual past life memory, then I was some sort of terrible creature. A vampire, perhaps? And Julian was my … lover? Husband? Or something more?

I remember how I felt about him. I'm feeling it now. Sweet, aching, giddy. Like nothing I've ever experienced. I'm terrified by the power he wields over me. I want to possess him, to live inside his skin.

I can't remember what he looked like, just the way he made me feel. The way he makes me feel.

I want to feel this way forever.

A dam bursts inside me as I sob into a sofa cushion. I've been alone my whole, sad life. Suddenly, I can't do it anymore. I want a man like Julian. And if I can't find one, I'll wither inside, little by little, a death of a thousand lonely moments.

A sobering fear grips me and the tears stop. What is happening? Yesterday I was fine—more or less—and now I'm a wreck, alternating wildly between love and despair. It has to be the drug. It's playing with my mind, making me lose control.

Before I can accept these feelings, I need to find out if Julian is real. I need to remember something about him that I can actually investigate and confirm. I leap from the sofa and pace, willing myself to remember. The minutes pass and nothing comes.

I need those pills, those black-and-white skunk pills that helped me remember, but I won't let that quack near me again. I'll have to *steal* the pills. I grab my keys and my backpack but stop at the door.

Wait, what's going on here? This is all happening so fast. I was just reading my mail and now I'm planning a break-in! Why am I acting so impulsively? Maybe it's the drug, but it feels like *something else,* something deeper.

I know the smart move is to stay at home, but to hell with that. I'm going to trust my instincts.

I'm still wearing the belted shirtdress and flats from my appointment with the shrink. Everything else I have is dirty. I decide to throw on my black beanie and jean jacket. Not exactly break-in attire.

It's past dark by the time the bus drops me off at Kennedy Plaza. High above, I see a shadow flit past the Superman building. Probably one of the peregrine falcons living up there. I hear they can hunt at night.

I'm relieved to find my shrink's building still open. Some of the businesses here have late hours, but not my shrink. I find his third-floor office closed and locked. I'm disappointed. I guess I was hoping for a note that read, "Emma, I've left the door unlocked. Your pills are on the counter."

The door has a keypad entry. After examining the pad, I see that three of the numbers are worn. How many combinations of those three buttons could there be? Screw it. I was never any good at math. I punch those three buttons in random combinations. To my surprise, the door unlocks almost immediately. Excellent security, Dr. Jekyll, but it was no match for my skilled burgling. If I'm not busy later, perhaps I should rob a bank.

As I open the door, I look down the carpeted hall and see the cleaning lady watching me. She is smiling, but inside she is nervous and suspicious. I offer her a lame explanation. "Left my purse in there. He said I could get it." *I don't carry one, of course, but she doesn't know that.*

She nods, eyeing my pack. Inside, she is getting angry. She sees this as *her* building.

I push inside the office.

There are a shocking number of pills in his small office. Pills for every neurosis and every orifice. There's really a suppository for bed-wetting? Lovely.

I've opened every bottle in his office. He's apparently running his own pharmacy here. Dozens of bottles now litter his teak desk, but not a single damn skunk pill to be found.

Out in the waiting room, I hear the door rattle open. A male voice calls out. "Hello?" It's security.

I spin, eyes wildly searching the office for some undiscovered cabinet. But I've looted them all. I hope the security guard will use his gun on me. It will be simpler than explaining this. Desperate, I notice Dr. Jekyll's hideous plaid sport coat hanging on a coat rack. I rush over and check the pockets.

Shit, the pills were here all along. The label on the bottle is unpronounceable, blahblahtine something.

Security Man pokes his nose into the office. Damn, he does have a gun. I'm relieved to see that his finger isn't on the trigger. "Miss, are you all right?" He looks young, with a drawn face and eyes dark from lack of sleep. Inside, he is worried for me. I guess chivalry isn't dead.

He will take these pills from me and I will lose my only way to remember more about Julian. Sure, I could swallow one before he got to me, but what would that accomplish? My previous memory didn't reveal much about Julian. I might have to take these pills for weeks to get the information I need.

The nice security man holds out his hand for the pills.

Julian, are you real or just a fantasy? Let's find out. I pop off the lid and gulp down the entire contents of the bottle. Tiny white sparks dance around me as I choke. I feel myself plunging down the rabbit hole.

Knight's Quest

STEFAN HILDEBRAND

Fear chews into my gut as I step through the bronze doors. I've never seen the Hall of Regents. I'm expecting the devil to jump out and snatch my soul.

But what I see is heaven: a Roman-style atrium with gushing fountains and floor mosaics. Gardens line the edges of the long, rectangular room. I don't recognize the flowers, mostly yellow and white. They smell like honey.

An artificial sun, created by a vast cluster of full-spectrum lights, keeps the gardens alive. At the far end of the atrium sits a stone portico supported by marble columns. A few people stand in its shadow, talking among themselves.

I keep my eyes unfocused as I enter, using my peripheral vision to check both sides of the door for potential attackers. Somehow, there's a breeze in here. I feel the fountain mist on my face. This is a room fit for an emperor.

As I cross the atrium, I study the mosaics on the floor. They look very old. I recognize several faces unknown to history, but well known to KoR: Quintilius, the Knight who killed the satyr pope, John XII; Costica Marica, who led the infamous vampire, Vlad Tepes, into a Turkish trap; and Warian, who killed the fierce Were king, Penda of Mercia. No doubt every famous Knight of Rome is immortalized in this atrium, a place where their faces are walked on as a lesson in humility.

My face will never be immortalized on this floor, but my blood soon might.

A neon-green hummingbird zips past as I approach the portico. Three people turn to observe me: my master, Henry Cobo, his white-bearded face solemn and unreadable; Preceptor Ericka Stockhausen, our Base Commander, wearing a black uniform that makes her blue eyes glow eerily; and a scowling, dwarfish man who could only be the National Commander, Albert Amedeo. What the hell is he doing here?

The Preceptor speaks with a forced smile. "Squire Hildebrand, today is a big day for you."

I have no idea what she's talking about. Best to keep my mouth shut.

She takes a step toward me, her voice lightening. "Your training is over."

Nine hard years of work have come to an end. I was expecting this. I should feel happy. So why do I feel this sense of impending doom?

The Preceptor isn't getting the reaction she expected. She lightens her tone even more. "We have a quest for you."

I nod my thanks. The quest is the final test. If I succeed, I'll be knighted.

Amedeo jumps in, impatient with the Preceptor's cheery tone. "It's a solo mission. No safety net. Tell no one, not even our own people. Report only to us."

I nod. *That's odd. Some kind of black op?*

Amedeo narrows his eyes at me. He's a foot shorter, pushing seventy, and looks like he could eat me for breakfast. "Your surveillance of Emma Rue is over. Bring her in for boxing."

My stomach burns. I bite back my urge to question the order. Emma isn't a paranormal. Why does she deserve deincarnation?

Master Cobo, as if reading my mind, speaks softly, his voice nearly swallowed by the burbling fountains. "Emma's mother was on our radar, so we've been keeping an eye on Emma as well. We've called you here because Emma has attacked a KoR operative working as a professor. We think she recognized him with soulsight. He's likely an enemy from one of her past lives."

Soulsight. That means Emma had once been a vampire. If soulsight becomes strong enough, the ability imprints itself on future incarnations. It only happens with the most powerful vampires, nobles in the Black Rose Society. Maybe Emma is one of them, and her vampire soul has started reasserting itself. Maybe that's why KoR has decided she must pay with her life, and all her future lives. But is that justice?

The Preceptor speaks, her voice formal now. "Squire Hildebrand, do you accept the quest?"

You don't say no to these people. "Yes, Preceptor."

Amedeo waves me away with a sharp gesture of his meaty hand.

I realize something as I walk back toward the bronze doors. Emma is a human girl with no allies. Capturing her will be the easiest Knight's Quest ever assigned. They must have given me the job because they don't want me taking any real risks in the field. My future is in the ludus. I'll be teaching Ars Duellica until my hair turns white, like Master Cobo. I guess that's good. People who work inside the walls of KoR get promoted. People who work outside them die.

Fate is a fickle bitch. I'm on the fast track to KoR leadership when I should already be dead. A mole in KoR is unheard of, much less a mole with a commission. This is my chance to become the highest-placed spy to ever infiltrate KoR, but only if I take out Emma. Could I do that to a girl I really like?

Sindóm

CASSANDRA CROSS

1814

EMMA'S PAST LIFE

Julian has made secret plans for our anniversary. My attempts to coax them from him have met with failure. We have been bloodmates for thirty-eight marvelous years and yet he remains a lovely enigma, ever able to surprise and delight. He nurtures an aura of mystery, not because he doesn't trust me, but because he loves me and knows how easily I grow bored. He is always in my thoughts, in my heart, his soul embracing mine.

I sit in my room before my lovely Adam-style mahogany vanity. Candlelight dances on the polished wood while Ida's dark fingers play a familiar melody on the silk strings of my pale stays. I feel a pinch from an ambitious tug (a rare misstep). She whispers in response, knowing the strength of my hearing. "Sorry, Mistress Cross."

I wave my hand. *"C'est rien."* Ida has been good to me

over the decades. The lines of time have furrowed her face while my skin has remained unmarked, and never once has she raised a complaint or made an inquiry. She loves me and accepts me for who I am. One day soon I will free her from the bondage of slavery.

In the giltwood mirror, I see my blonde hair wrapped in coils around my finger. One day I must rid myself of this girlish habit.

⚜

I await Julian in the Great Hall. Long red curtains made of Chinese silk frame the tall, moonlit windows. Ten yards above my head the great dome rises, with a moon and stars twinkling in a gilded paint.

When we first built this home in Newport, Julian insisted that I name it. I called it *Refuge d'Amoureux*. Our love grew stronger over the decades but our refuge began to age, so Julian brought over Mr. John Nash from London to rebuild it. The architect cost a bloody fortune but his services were well worth the coin.

The hall's boldest feature is a painting by Julian. He painted all of the pieces that hang in our manse, but this is my favorite. To the mortal eye it appears as nothing more than a blur of colorful clouds. But Julian's palette includes blaze paints, created from ground blazestone, visible only to Transcendent eyes. It is a painting of my soul, and if you watch for long enough, it appears to move. If Julian St. Fleur were mortal, his work would hang in the world's greatest museums. But the risk of exposure is too great for his paintings to be seen beyond these walls.

I fuss with my dress, fluttered layers of white silk. It feels odd to have the bodice so close to the bust, but all the fashionable ladies now prefer this high-waisted style. I do enjoy the bare arms. Scandalous!

A few of our Irish servants hover about, cleaning and whatnot. Irish are quite popular now, especially among the abolitionists. They part to make way for Julian as he descends the stairs. Their eyes follow him with admiration and envy. He is, and will always remain, the most beautiful man I have ever seen, both in body and soul.

His rose-gold eyes, in a perpetual sunset, gaze at me from across the room. I can see that he approves of my dress. I feel his invisible third hand on the fabric, touching me here, and there, and in places best left for later. I whisper to him. "We mustn't be late."

He nods as he adjusts his pale lavender cravat, the silk radiant against his midnight-blue waistcoat. I'm pleased to see he hasn't brought his hat. I love to see every lock of his long, caramel hair. It has a way of swimming in the breeze.

We join our third hands and he leads me to him. He places a gentle kiss on my cheek, taking care not to disturb my paints and powders. A pale look is fashionable but I still need a bit of color.

He puts his hand around my waist and we walk into the foyer. I smile at the pair of mahogany chairs I've just acquired. Lion's-paw feet, with cushions upholstered in a silk-and-wool fabric embossed with subtle leopard spots.

Positively savage!

An Irish girl with long black hair casts her eyes to the floor as she opens the front doors. A month ago, her friend, one of our cooks, had the audacity to touch Julian's hand in passing. Now that friend is gone, and the Irish are keeping their hands and eyes to themselves. I won't share my beloved with anyone.

Julian and I pass through the sturdy pair of cypress doors with beveled glass windows framed in iron. I smell the spicy scent of their wood as we enter the night's embrace.

Once outside, Julian draws me out of the silver-blue moonlight and into a pool of shadow behind a marble column.

Again, he has surprised me. "No carriage?"

He shakes his head. "Our destination is much too far for a carriage. We'll be meeting one of my … associates … in Washington. He'll be joining us for dinner at the White House."

It takes me a moment to understand. He means the home of President Madison! This will mean a shadow walk, and I fear my yellow court shoes are too delicate for the journey. Julian knows my thoughts.

"It's only an hour's run, my love. I'll carry your shoes if you like."

I hadn't realized he was planning such an adventure. Dinner with the President. How on earth had he managed that? I show him a smile. "Thank you, but I can manage my shoes."

He bows and extends his hand. I take it and we slip into Velox, disappearing from the mortal world.

Julian and I stand on a hill overlooking Washington. The war has taken a turn for the worse. Under the half-moon we can see Redcoats sacking the city. They look like angry sparks, drifting from building to building, setting fire to everything in their path.

Dinner was unmemorable. We met with Hunfrid Gurker, a somewhat disreputable art dealer Julian has done business with in the past. Julian was supposed to introduce him to the President, remuneration for some previous deal they had made. But the introduction had been a brief, hurried affair along the road while the President and his wife Dolley were escaping town.

President Madison is a wisp of a man with an odd nose and no conversational skills. But his soul is pure, and I like his wife, Dolley. Her carriage was brimming with antiques she was saving from the British.

After the rushed meeting, the dealer slipped Julian a small package, now under his waistcoat. I know it's a gift for me. And Julian knows that I know. After making me wait, he finally smiles and produces the present. "I have a confession. We really didn't come to meet the President. We came to acquire this from Hunfrid." He presses it into my hands, a long, slim box.

I gasp in delight as I see faint colors swirling inside. Whatever it is, it has a soul! I open the box and discover a thin dagger forged of some dark green metal rippled with blazestone inlay. Emeralds sparkle in the handle. The blade glints wickedly in the moonlight, promising death, or something worse than death.

Julian wraps an arm around my shoulders. "It's very old, pre-classical, likely forged by elves in the Age of Dragons. And it has a name. *Síndóm.*"

I draw Síndóm from the box. I know it is a "she." Her handle is warm in my hand. She seems to purr. I see strange runes inscribed on her blade.

)((𝕯ᕤ𝕆𝕆

"What do these symbols mean?"

Julian's voice grows serious. "I've no idea, my love. But take care. The weapon has some exotic power that no one can fathom."

Tears flood my eyes. This is a gift beyond value, heavy with the ancient history of the Fae Folk. And it is *alive*. My voice wavers as I whisper, "*Je t'aime.*" I lean up to kiss him. As our lips touch, a shot rings out in the night, and then another—musket fire.

As we look to the city, we see fires everywhere. Suddenly, a half-dozen mounted dragoons swarm around the empty White House (only a half-mile away), thrusting burning torches through the shattered windows.

Julian and I remain calm. I am a general's daughter, and we have both seen the worst war has to offer. Besides, this is a rare opportunity to watch history in the making. Will this mean the collapse of the fragile union?

Carefully, I return the formidable dagger to its box. The weapon radiates power and mystery, but I must explore it another time. "Those dragoons are headed this way."

Julian peers toward the burning White House. "I believe you're correct. Shall we fend them off together?"

Sometimes, it's difficult to tell when he's joking.

Gigglemeister

Emma Rue

THE PRESENT

I OPEN MY EYES and find myself in a hospital room. I close them again, trying to cling to the dream of being Cassandra and having Julian at my side in Washington. It was magnificent. This world cannot compare. If it was a dream, it was the most remarkable dream of my life, a romantic fantasy beyond compare. But if it wasn't just a dream, if it was real, it shatters my understanding of the world. So I have to know the truth about Julian and Refuge d'Amoureux.

I open my eyes again and focus on the hospital bed. Memories of my arrival here flood back. I overdosed on those regression pills. My right nostril hurts where they ran the tube to send charcoal into my stomach. I kept gagging when they tried to put it in through my mouth. But the tube does nothing to hide the hospital's antiseptic smell; it's thick enough to taste.

I'm in Rhode Island Hospital. Probably their loony ward. My door is open. I hear a monitor beeping in the room next door and a half-dozen voices in the hall. An old man walks by pushing an IV stand on wheels. His hospital gown is open in the back and he isn't wearing underwear. What a wonderful place; charcoal up the nose and a free show.

My shrink came by earlier. I was kind of hazy at the time, but I remember that he won't be pressing charges for the break-in. I don't think he wants to explain his illicit pharmacy to the police.

I'm under observation and a social worker is coming soon. I know the drill. They're worried I'm acting out, that taking the pills was a suicidal gesture. At least that's something they understand. If I told them the real reason I took those pills they would put me in a straitjacket.

Melita is just down the hall. I hear her youngest daughter, Kaya, singing one of her made-up songs. "You got warts in your shorts, warts in your shorts. Warts and shorts, warts and shorts."

Kaya has a habit of creating odd and embarrassing songs. That's part of why I love her. The other reason is that she is like me, cast aside by her real mother. Melita's younger sister was a drug addict who abandoned Kaya. Thankfully, Melita was there to save the precocious girl. Kaya thinks of Melita as her mom now.

I hear the concern in Melita's voice as she talks to the doctor. She is the only person in my life who worries about me. But she's also got worries of her own, so I hate to upset her.

Melita enters my hospital room alone. Melita's older daughter, Seble, must be watching Kaya. Melita wants to make sure I'm not a raving lunatic before she brings the kids in to see me. I push aside the foul-smelling pudding they've left for me and do my best to smile.

Poor Melita looks squeezed into her blue pantsuit. I want to take her clothes shopping, but neither of us can afford it. On the surface, she is all smiles, but beneath that I see the colors of fear. I need to reassure her. "I'm fine, Melita. It was just a memory drug, not crack."

She hugs me and touches me on the nose, her signature way of saying *I love you*. She still hasn't spoken. She sits beside the bed and takes my hand. Her palm is warm and soft, her fingers strong. A mother's hand. Not that I would know.

She has a way of getting me to talk first. "I'm sorry to worry *you*."

"I'm fine, just fine, you just focus on getting better. I'm dropping the kids with Nana so I can cover your shift tonight."

"Thank you." Melita thinks that I will be in the hospital for a while. But I'm not sticking around to talk to that social worker. I have a plan. And if Melita catches wind of it, she'll make them cuff me to the bed.

She has some of her purple lipstick on her front teeth. I rub my own teeth to alert her and she wipes it off and speaks without missing a beat. "Why a memory drug? What were you trying to remember?"

I need to tell someone. At least a little of it. "Do you believe in past lives?"

Her eyebrows rise. "I once read a book about it at the library."

"When I took the pills, I dreamed I was wearing gorgeous dresses, living in a mansion." *She doesn't need to know the vampire part of the story.*

Melita sizes me up. "These pills, what was in them?"

"I don't know. But the dream was vivid, like an actual memory."

Worry clouds her face. "There's a thin line between dreams and memory."

"You never answered my question. Past lives. True, or just what we want to believe?"

She thinks it over. "The book said that souls kind of orbit around each other, so you're constantly interacting with people from your past lives. That's why we sometimes really like or really hate people we just met, because we're remembering a past life connection. That part makes a certain amount of sense."

Hmm, I liked Melita from the moment I met her. Her soul looks familiar and comforting. Perhaps Cassandra knew one of Melita's past incarnations. And perhaps Cassandra had met Professor Leeks in one of his past lives. "Have you ever felt like you've known someone before?"

Melita slowly nods. "There was another interesting thing. The book said that odd habits you have in this life are caused by things that happened in your past life. Like people who refuse to drive because they once died in a car accident."

I've always been afraid of big dogs. Was I once attacked by one?

Suddenly, Kaya charges into the room. Last month she lost one of her baby teeth, and she smiles in a way that shows off the gap. She crouches at the foot of my bed, peeks over the rail, and squeaks a question. "Who am I?" She never tires of this game.

"You're Betsy Ross."

Kaya giggles and shakes her head, sending her beaded braids flying around her face.

"You're Martha Washington."

She laughs and shakes her head again.

"You're Kaya Gigglemeister, Queen of Asa Messer Elementary School."

"Yes!" She grabs my feet through the sheets and gleefully shakes them.

Melita flashes her a stern expression. "Play nice."

I love Kaya. She's always so happy. I want to know her secret.

Seble enters the room, wearing black sunglasses and a haggard look no teenager should have. "Sorry, she slipped out while we were in the bathroom."

Seble gathers up her squirming cousin without looking at me. Kaya is fine, but seeing me in a hospital bed is scaring Seble, who is hiding behind those sunglasses. I want to say something to her, but I don't know what. She checks the time on her phone. "Mom, we're late for Nana's."

Melita nods. "Go on out to the car. I'll catch up."

Seble hurries out with Kaya, who waves goodbye to me.

Melita's eyes lock onto mine, her expression intense. "What if something bad happened in your past life, something that drove you into this hospital bed? Is that really a memory you want to dredge up?"

I have no answer for her.

Melita touches me on the nose again. "I'll come by after work."

"I might be released before then."

"You need money for the bus home?"

"I'm good, Melita, thanks."

She nods and reluctantly turns away. After a long look back, she's finally out the door.

Alone now, I slip from the bed. I'm wearing a hospital gown, and (thankfully) underwear. I dig around the room and find my flats, shirtdress, and jean jacket. The beanie is missing in action.

I need to make my escape from this place. Melita is probably right; I should let it go. But I can't. I have to know if Cassandra and Julian are real.

Trickster

STEFAN HILDEBRAND

After receiving my assignment to capture Emma, I drove four straight hours, speeding most of the way, to reach this lonely stretch of Vermont forest. Lucky I didn't get a ticket. Pinecones crunch underfoot as I step out of my car and disappear into the trees, following trails no untrained eye can see. This is the back way into Corby, a longer route that gives me a chance to reconnect with the forest. I'm excited by the sharp smell of spruce trees, mixed with a few pines and hemlocks. I feel like a kid again. It makes me remember a simpler life, growing up in these woods before it all went to shit.

It's been a year since I last invoked. That's a long time for an *Ulfhedinn*. My spirit wolf, whose name cannot be pronounced by the human tongue, is pissed because I've ignored Him for so long. So I don't know if He will come. This wolf is strong and proud. Like all of the wolves our people channel, He is a *vargr*, a horse-sized wolf descended from Fenrir, a giant beast that defied the Norse gods.

The *Ulfhednar* all have a special tattoo, made in part from the blood of a wolf. Mine is on my scalp, hidden by my hair. KoR hasn't found it, which is why I'm still alive. It's a growling wolf with red eyes. The tattoo tingles as I reach out to Him. *I'm sorry it's been so long.*

After my blót, the ceremony that bonded my wolf to me, my father said something weird. He said that my wolf had taken a while to come to me. He didn't say why and I didn't ask. I was a frightened thirteen-year-old feeling the power of the Were for the first time. It was overwhelming. A lot of kids piss themselves. But ever since my dad said that, I've wondered if my wolf had been hesitant to bond with me. Maybe I don't measure up.

He is coming, but He's taking his time. He wants to make a point. If it was life or death, He would already be here. I hope so anyway.

It's been five years since I last made contact with my people, Clan Corby. Our kind are descended from Northmen, the Ulfhednar, who channel the wolf in battle. Farther north of here lies another town, one in the hands of the *Berserkir,* who invoke the bear. What makes us Were is the ability to bond with animal spirits. The power is passed along family lines.

I reel as the hundreds of forest scents suddenly overwhelm me. *He* is here. His spirit coexisting inside me. I must be careful to stay out of sight. Anyone stumbling upon me would see my menacing frost-blue eyes, my gray pointed ears, my huge, bone-white canine teeth, and the long pale claws on my left hand. My wolf leaves human fingers on my right hand so I can use a gun.

I haven't changed size or *transformed* as most people would think. There was no painful shifting of my body and I'm still wearing my clothes. It's as if He stepped inside me. But people who know me would still recognize me. It's not like I'm down on all fours and covered with fur.

I wince as everything gets louder. Chirping birds sound like sirens. I hear the scurry of every rabbit and mouse. And finally, the shadows disappear as my eyes become more sensitive to light. The shafts of sunlight that separate the trees burn like bolts of lightning.

He wants to run. So I run. The ground blurs at my feet as I shoot through the trees. As always, I'm filled with anger. No one knows why that happens, but every Ulfhedinn learns to control it when they invoke. I also feel a sense of awe as I fly through the forest without even breathing hard. Whatever happens to my body—exhaustion, pain, injury—is absorbed by Him.

I uninvoke my wolf as I near Corby. The anger subsides. I don't feel any physical change, but my body instantly returns to normal as He leaves me.

Ahead I spot the "claw," its giant steel pincers hanging high in the late afternoon sun. The massive claw picks up a bundle of raw logs from a truck and swings them onto the stacks. From there, the logs will be processed by Corby's hungry lumber mill, staffed by three shifts working twenty-four hours a day.

I was never a great logger because my mind was always on school. My father, our clan leader, didn't mind that I was crap with a chainsaw. He wanted me to see the big picture. He wanted me to run this town. That was, until KoR recruited me.

As I pass the old wooden schoolhouse, I can't resist looking in through the window. I see that Ms. Lystad is still teaching, wearing her trademark bun. I had a thing for her as a kid. Damn, she's getting old. Guess I am too.

Ms. Lystad spots me and waves me in as if she had been expecting me all along. Nothing ever rattled her, and I remember trying. When we put a rat snake in her desk drawer, she took it out and spent the rest of the day lecturing us on ophiology. There was a test afterward and I got the top score. Ms. Lystad wanted me to go on to college but KoR had other plans.

Ms. Lystad motions me to the front of the room. "Welcome, Mr. Hildebrand. You can join us for a lesson on Futhorc."

I survey the kids and see them drawing Anglo-Saxon runes on paper. They didn't teach that when I was here, but there was talk about it. Some of the folks in town wanted to turn this into a Scandinavian immersion school.

Ms. Lystad takes my arm as if I'm still a kid. "Class, this is Stefan Hildebrand, a former student. Who can spell *Stefan* using the runes?"

A pale kid raises his hand.

Ms. Lystad smiles encouragement. "Good, Erik, write it on the board."

With the forests disappearing and loggable trees getting harder to come by, Corby is a poor town. They don't have a lot of computers and such. Any of the KoR agents would burst out laughing if they saw Erik pick up that dusty stub of chalk. We would seem like rednecks to them.

Erik carefully draws out my name in the runes…

My dyslexia makes the characters swim. For one strange moment, they seem to spell *traitor*.

My mom rushes out of our modest house as I approach. She hugs me hard enough to hurt. I see that her chestnut hair now has streaks of gray. I feel like some sort of time traveler, thrown forward into my own future. "Hi, Mom."

She doesn't answer. She goes silent when she's really happy or really sad. As she pulls me inside the house, I realize they've painted the aluminum siding a lighter shade of green.

I barely recognize my family home. Strange how it seems so small now. My dad's lumberjack trophies have disappeared from the mantel, replaced by Mom's butterfly collection, mostly swallowtails and brushfoots. I never liked that hobby. Once they die, they're not pretty anymore. "Where's Dad?"

"Already on his way." She sounds nervous. Something is wrong. I take a closer look at the place. None of my dad's stuff is around. Did they get a divorce? Why would they do that?

My father enters the house. He looks thinner than I remember but hasn't grayed much. He shakes my hand and I feel the calluses of a working man. We don't hug. We've never been huggers, except for the one time I fell in the river as a kid. He hugged me when they pulled me out. Whenever I doubt his love for me, I remember that one and only hug.

His tone seems guarded. "Good to see you. Everything okay?"

Mom pops her head in from the kitchen. "You two have a seat. I'm making dinner."

Definitely a divorce. She's telling him to sit in what used to be his own house. Shit, I don't have time to deal with this now. I catch my dad's wary eye. "We need to talk, and then I have to run."

He nods and we sit. I choose a spot by the fireplace, a low stool carved from a maple stump. Suddenly, I'm not sure how to proceed. "Um, you see, there's this girl."

And suddenly Mom pops her head in again. "What's her name?"

"Emma Rue."

Dad's pale eyes narrow. "She's *Osterkligr?*" Osterkligr means *weak*. It's a derogatory term for all those who are not Were.

"Yes. She was a vampire in her past life and KoR has ordered me to bring her in for boxing. If I do, they'll make me a Knight."

Mom's face turns hard.

Dad sighs and his shoulders drop. His way of showing annoyance. "How much does she know about you?"

"Nothing. She thinks my name is Micah, that I'm an ex-soldier attending college."

Mom speaks quietly. "You like this girl."

It isn't a question. Maybe she's worried I want to mate with Emma. By law, Were only mate with Were. I need to be direct now. "I want out of KoR. I want to come home. And I want Corby to help Emma find another life, some-where safe."

Dad says nothing. Mom, worry lines creasing her face, heads back into the kitchen. But I know she's still listening.

My fingernails pick at the maple stool. I decide to fill the growing silence. "I'm sorry—I'm just not built to shed innocent blood. You didn't raise me that way."

My dad stares out the window, seeming to count the spruce trees in the forest beyond. He does that when he's thinking. After a long time, his fiery eyes turn back to me. "We live like animals, Stefan, hiding out in the woods because the Knights of Rome want to kill every last one of us. Women, minorities, gay people, they're all winning their right to exist as equals in our society. But where are *our* rights, Stefan? Why can't *we* live in the open? I want a better world for us, but that won't happen until KoR is destroyed. You're our best chance of making that happen. The future of our people is on your shoulders. So do whatever it takes to become a Knight."

Suddenly, I feel the weight of my clan, pressing me into the earth, smothering my existence. Somehow I thought my dad would side with his own son. I should have known better. It wasn't my idea to join KoR in the first place; I just wanted to go to college. But when KoR unknowingly tried to recruit one of their sworn enemies, Corby couldn't pass up the opportunity to let them, so my life changed forever.

I nearly invoke as someone suddenly pounds on the front door.

Dad frowns and gets up to answer it. He throws open the door, revealing Neil Torp, the Summoner. He looks like he's gained about a hundred pounds of crazy since officiating my blót. His gray hair is spiky. His green eyes look too big for his face and half his mouth is hanging limp. When he speaks, he slurs so badly I can't understand him. He used to be so wise and full of life. What the hell happened?

Mom re-enters the room and whispers in my ear. "Stroke. And now dementia."

Poor bastard. I extend my hand to him. "Hello, Mr. Torp, good to see you again, sir."

He throws his arms around me as if falling. He smells like cheap cologne and even cheaper liquor. He slurs something I can't understand and immediately goes into convulsions.

Dad gets on the phone and calls Corby's volunteer fire department. There's always an EMT on duty. In a logging town, they get a lot of work.

As I ease Mr. Torp to the ground, his twitching body suddenly goes limp. Somehow, I know he is dead.

My mother looks down at him with a mixture of pity and confusion.

Maybe she understood his final, slurred words. "What did he say?"

She shakes her head. "I'm not sure. Something about a *trickster.*"

Kiss Behind the Bakery

CASSANDRA CROSS

1775

EMMA'S PAST LIFE

My father, recently promoted to a general in the Continental Army, looks as hale and hearty as I have ever seen him. Sweat gleams from his grinning face as his ax flies, chopping wood for the hearth. Of course we have slaves for that, but he enjoys the work.

He catches my eye as I cross our proper English lawn, kept in check by a menagerie of grazing goats and sheep. A carriage, drawn by a pair of fine black Friesians, awaits me at the stable for my weekly trip into town. But something in Father's face tells me the trip will be postponed. "Cassie! Walk with me!"

He hugs me as I approach and touches me on the nose, a gesture of affection that has persisted since my childhood.

We walk to a swing bench he built when I was a girl. It

hangs from two iron chains connected to a massive oak branch. We sit and he kicks his feet, causing the bench to swing. I don't think I've ever seen him so happy. For some reason, it worries me. "You're in a fine mood, Father."

"Indeed I am. Do you remember my dear friend Captain Thomas Tulley?"

I do. But I can hardly tell my father why. *Last year Tom and I kissed behind the Sharpson Bakery in Newport.* "I have a vague recollection of him."

"You may not be aware, but he's quite taken with you."

Oh no. Please do not continue down this path.

His eyes look far away and his face grows suddenly grave. "Tom is the bravest man I've ever known. There are things in war, my dear, terrible things that men don't speak of with their womenfolk."

"I'm not a delicate flower, Father. You know you can tell me anything." *Why did I say that? Something tells me I don't want to hear what's coming.*

He mulls over my words, watching a bee circle a burgundy spire of hollyhocks brought over from England. In his eyes, I am like that delicate flower. Is Tom to be my bee?

Just when I think he'll remain silent, Father begins to speak, his eyes avoiding mine. "When the British began their third assault, we ran out of ammunition and I called the retreat to Cambridge. We lost significant numbers traveling over Bunker Hill. The 63rd Foot was pressing when my horse was shot out from under me. I rolled into a ravine. By the time I crawled out, I was behind their line, and the

British were killing our wounded. Many of their officers were dead and their soldiers had fallen into a rage. As I watched good men, men who could have recovered, die at their hands, I thought of…"

As he stutters to a stop, I see tears rolling down his cheeks. I am stunned and frightened. I have never seen my father cry. I reach out and take his hand, and after a moment, he continues.

"I thought of you, the light of my life. I thought of missing your wedding, of never being a grandfather to your children. I thought of all the fatherly promises I would never keep. And then I saw Tom, who had refused to abandon me in the field. The British fired at him a dozen times as he crossed that bloody ground to save me. And by God's grace, he survived unscathed, leading me into a creek bed where we made our escape. Thanks to Tom, I will be able to keep those promises I made to you."

I know where this is going. I don't love Tom. But how can I say that to my weeping father? His tears have become my own.

"Tom has asked for your hand, and I've given him my blessing. You won't find a better man in all of New England."

This has played out exactly as I feared. I find my tongue paralyzed and the silence grows between us.

The sweet smell of spiced cider and pumpkin casserole drifts across the crowded garden. The Reverend John

Graves, the rector of King's Church in Providence, directs the final preparations like a fussy field marshal. He is Tom's minister and I'm told that it's a great honor to have him presiding. Reverend Graves is not pleased that I've chosen to have the wedding at our home, but was mollified when we published our banns at his church as well as my own. A part of me hoped that these public declarations of our intent to marry would attract an objection, but after a month, we heard nothing, and the marriage was approved.

As I stand at the edge of the garden, Amity Claridge, my best friend from childhood, adjusts the collar on my blue wool gown. "Please Cassie, just a small hint."

"I'm not telling you where Mother hid that piece of nutmeg!" *I didn't mean to snap at her. I feel very ill at ease.*

Amity grins. "Fine, I'll simply eat your entire wedding cake to find it. It's either that or die an old maid."

She thinks I'm nervous and seeks to put me at ease. But I'm closer to horrified than nervous. How did it come to this? A dozen times I tried to tell Father no, and a dozen times I failed. Tom is a wonderful man, tall and handsome, fiercely brave. Every girl in Newport has pictured herself with him, and he has chosen *me*. So why am I not drawn to him?

I think back to our kiss behind the bakery. He pressed me against the wall, wanting more, but I had nothing to give him. I was flattered by his attention but in my heart I knew he would never be my one true love. That man remains undiscovered.

Across the garden I hear Tom's soldier friends, already

drunk, joking that he's only getting married to avoid the bachelor's tax. But they all know it isn't true. Tom is in love. And I feel the weight of his love pressing down on me, making it impossible to breathe.

A violin begins to play. This is all happening so fast. Amity says something but I can't hear her. I realize that Father has taken my arm and is walking me down the brick garden path that leads to Tom and Reverend Graves. I can smell the lavender that mother grows in the garden. She dries it and tucks it into our clothes when she puts them away.

Suddenly, I feel so light that I look down to make certain my feet are still on the ground. All of the sounds and smells and colors of the wedding overwhelm me. I see the world through two tiny pinpricks of light. Only Father's steady arm is keeping me on my feet. He says something, I have no idea what, but I do my best to smile and nod, moving ever forward.

In a few moments, my life will change forever. Perhaps for the better, but I think not. All I need to do is collapse in Father's arms, and it will be over. They will stop the ceremony. If I am to do that, I must do it now.

Rusted Key

EMMA RUE

THE PRESENT

I WAKE UP on a crowded Route 60 RIPTA bus. I fell asleep in my seat and we're already in Newport. I hope the answers I'm looking for are here.

Cassandra's life, real or imagined, is a little confusing. The dreams aren't coming in chronological order. Fortunately, my knowledge of history is helping me make sense of them. Tom must be a man that Cassandra met before Julian. Had poor Cassandra gone through with the wedding? How did she end up meeting Julian? So many unanswered questions, including the biggest one: Is all this even real?

I step off the bus and into Newport, smelling the salt air. Providence has its charms—I love going to Waterfire—but Newport is a journey into the past. As a little girl I imagined that I'd live here one day.

I head south from the bus station and pass by Bannister's

Wharf. I catch a whiff of freshly steamed cherrystone clams. My stomach rumbles and I'm tempted to stop, but I have to save my money for the mansion tours. So instead, I head down Thames Street and cut over to the shipyard to see if I can spot any yachts. I'm disappointed to find the docks mostly empty.

When I was younger, St. Mary's brought us to Newport on a field trip. I remember there being a nice bookshop not far from here, Spring Street Bookstore, but I know better than to go there. I'll get sucked in, and I'm on a mission. I need to find Refuge d'Amoureux, Cassandra's beautiful mansion from my dream.

I've spent some of my dwindling cash on a self-guided audio tour of The Breakers, the most opulent of the Gilded Age mansions. Constructed by the Vanderbilt family in the late nineteenth century, the sprawling house has seventy rooms. They called it a summer "cottage"! Such humble people. Salt of the earth.

I walk through the vast mansion and enter the library, gasping in delight. In my headphones, the tour guide mentions the dolphin painted on the ceiling. I hadn't noticed that on my trip through here with Saint Mary's. My eyes must have been glued to the walnut bookshelves and their gold-leaf trim. They've got the area roped off, so I can't get close enough to read the titles. Pity. I have a fetish for leather-bound books.

I think of my bookshelves made of cinder blocks and

wooden planks. My entire apartment could fit into this one beautiful library room. If Cassandra could see my apartment, she would think it a prison cell. What was it like, living in a mansion, surrounding by all this luxury? Did it spoil her? How could it not?

I realize that I'm thinking about Cassandra as if she were a real person. I pray that she was, because if she wasn't, I may be losing my mind.

A group passes by in the middle of a guided tour. I abandon my headphones and slip into the back of the crowd, trying to look like I belong. Another fifteen minutes into the tour and I see an opening for my question. The guide, a snow-haired woman with painted-on eyebrows, is talking about other mansions in the area. I raise my hand and speak. "I've heard of another mansion, Refuge d'Amoureux. What can you tell us about it?"

Eyebrow lady frowns. She knows very well that I'm not part of her tour. "Young lady, I'm afraid there's no such property."

"Early nineteenth century, rebuilt by John Nash?"

She laughs haughtily. "If a Nash was in Newport, it would likely be on the circuit. Where did you get your information?" She's angry now. I've challenged her expertise. In a moment she'll ask to see my tour receipt. Or else she'll pluck out my eyes with her spindly fingers.

"Must have read it somewhere. Sorry to interrupt." I wave an apology and head for the exit.

ᴄᴏᴏ♡ᴏᴏ

By sunset, my flats are killing me and hunger pinches my stomach. I've trudged along the length of the breezy Cliff Walk, trying to think of where else to look. I've seen the outside of every mansion on the tour circuit. It's almost dark and I've encountered nothing that matches my memory of Refuge d'Amoureux.

Maybe this is all for nothing. Maybe Cassandra and Julian are a drug-induced hallucination. Damn those skunk pills. Are they affecting my judgment? Have I gone crazy?

I struggle to think. Maybe Cassandra's mansion was torn down. Or maybe just renovated beyond recognition. Another thought suddenly gives me hope. All of the mansions in the circuit were taken over by the Preservation Society of Newport County when they became too expensive for their owners to maintain. But any homes still in *private* possession would not be on the tour. But how would I find them? I'd have to check the city property records, and of course their office would be closed by now. If I carried a phone I could check online. Then again, if I carried a phone it would be broken by now.

Depression overwhelms me as I sit on the Forty Steps leading down to the water. A red-gold sun sets behind me, casting long shadows over Easton Bay. I remember these steps from my first visit here. This is where the Irish servants used to party after they finished a long day of working in these huge mansions. I imagine a lot of drinking was involved.

I see a city worker with filthy leather gloves pulling garbage from a public rubbish bin. I want to enjoy the water, but I can't take my eyes off this man. I have an idea. "Excuse me, may I ask you a question?"

He looks up, shocked that his invisibility has been broken. His mouth forms an "O" between his mustache and scraggly beard.

"Sorry to bother you, but I'm looking for a mansion that may be off the circuit."

The sanitation worker, Carlson, turned out to be a sweetie. He gave me a bottle of water that I consumed in one long drink. He hadn't heard of Refuge d'Amoureux, but he got on his radio and talked to his supervisor. There wasn't any mansion with that name, but there was a run-down property with a big house that somewhat matched my description. Carlson dropped me off at the edge of the property, where I now stand, because he isn't allowed to drive on private roads.

The sun has disappeared and it's nearly dark. I stand alone at the end of a broken road that snakes under a canopy of drooping trees. I don't see any mansion. To find it, I will have to walk down this road and into the gloomy tunnel formed by the overhanging trees. I'm picturing the headline: "Expelled Student Found Dead in Secluded Area."

As I enter the tree tunnel, it grows so dark that I can barely see my feet. Something smells sour. Tree branches touch my shoulders as if reaching to strangle me.

After what seems like an eternity, I emerge from the trees and see the dim outline of a ramshackle mansion. My heart sinks. This is *not* the place. It has the wrong kind of doors, three levels instead of two, and there's nothing but dead grass where the stone carriageway should be.

In the stillness I hear the chirp of crickets. Not a single light shines from the mansion. It lies before me in the night like a decomposed body. I should leave now. But it's dark, getting cold, and I have no phone and not enough money for the bus. Perhaps I can find a blanket inside, or some canned food.

I creep toward the broken mansion as if it were a big dog, ready to bite. As I step past the entry columns, I see something wedged in the crack between the double doors. A paper of some sort. I pluck it out, stepping to the side of the porch to catch a ray of blue moonlight. It's a notice from the city, nearly five months old. Something about property taxes. It's addressed to "Richard Sinclair."

I'm convinced the place is empty, but I decide to knock, just to be sure. The steel knocker hangs askew from one screw, but it gets the job done. The knock goes unanswered, so I try the door handle. It's locked, of course. I try the handle again, hoping for a different result. *Stupid.* It doesn't open.

I pull my jean jacket tight around me. I'm shivering from the cold and my stomach aches from hunger. There's got to be a way inside. Perhaps a key is hidden somewhere. I check under the mat and find a brittle envelope. I carry it into the moonlight and peer at the front. The envelope has probably been out here for years, and at some point has gotten soaked. There's a single word on the front of the envelope, hard to make out...

Cassandra

I feel my heart stop. I'm at the right house, and Cassandra is real!

Relief overwhelms me as I realize I haven't gone mad. My fingers tremble as I open the envelope. The paper inside is molded and the ink has run together. Whatever message was in here is now unreadable. My heart sinks.

Then I find something else inside the envelope. A rusted key!

I hurry to push the key into the lock of the front door. It doesn't fit! I'm on an emotional rollercoaster. I just want to get off. I sit on the edge of the porch, hugging myself against the cold. I'm getting lightheaded from hunger.

Think, Emma, think. This key obviously opens *something*. A different door?

I get to my feet and walk around the side of the menacing mansion. Bushes and brambles have claimed the property. I feel briers scratching my ankles.

Behind the house squats some sort of Gothic tomb, its door guarded by two stone angels, their faces veiled by vines. The tomb door has no handle, no keyhole. I feel oddly drawn to this crypt, but there is no obvious way inside.

I turn to the back of the house. Trees block the moonlight, so I trace my hand along the wall to find my way. I discover a narrow door made of rusted iron. Maybe a servant's entrance?

The door is locked. I try the key. It fits but it won't turn. Shit! I can't take any more of this. I try the key again, wiggling it a bit and praying for a different result. And this time it turns the lock! My heart races as I pull open the creaking door. A pungent scent of decay washes over me and bile rises in my throat. If there was food in here, it's gone bad.

My shivering grows more violent. I'm not sure it's from the cold. I realize my finger has curled deep into my hair. At this moment, I would trade every lock of it for a flashlight. Part of me says it would be madness to step inside. Better to take my chances in the cold and try to make it back to civilization. But another part of me realizes that the mystery of my past, the mystery of Julian, lies inside these decaying walls.

I hear my heart thumping wicked hard as I step across the threshold, feeling my way into utter darkness.

Sleepcooking

CYNTHIA GREENE

It's surprisingly easy for a ghost to find Emma Rue. I just need to use someone like Carey Devors, a single mother working as an administrative assistant at Rhode Island College. When she's not updating student records, she's reading salacious romance novels on her computer screen, right next to a picture of her bucktoothed little boy. Her bald boss, sitting in the office across from her, has no idea.

This particular novel, *The King's Stable Girl*, is quite coarse. I watch through Carey's eyes as she eagerly approaches the end of the book. The libidinous king decides to marry the stable girl and make her his queen. But I imagine a different ending, and Carey sees my words on the page. Before the king can place the ring on the girl's finger, an assassin leaps from behind the throne and murders him. Now that's what I call a good read. Carey doesn't take it well. She cries a bit before closing the book on the screen.

I used to track down negligent parents for a living, so

finding Emma should be no problem, especially if Carey helps. I make her imagine that her phone is ringing, and when she picks up, I make her hear someone saying that Emma Rue's computer records are missing. Carey's ridiculous nail polish flashes with glitter as she taps her computer keys and checks for Emma's information on her screen.

Now I have Emma's address. Thank you, Carey.

After riding in the heads of a few postal workers, I find Emma's building, a run-down tenement in a bad part of Providence. These places attract gangs like a slut attracts syphilis.

Across the hall from Emma's apartment I find a nosy neighbor, a dirty old man who spends a shocking amount of time peering through his peephole. This is fortunate because I can't *compel* him to look through the peephole. Ghosts, for the most part, cannot control human bodies. That is the business of demons. But there is a loophole, one I will exploit, as soon as I can find a child in the building.

Rowan's plan is to capture Emma's soul, just as she did mine. Apparently, in her past life, Emma acquired a dagger that belonged to Rowan, and now the witch wants it back. I must kill Emma so that Rowan can intercept her soul and force her to divulge the location of the weapon. Rowan prefers having ghosts like me do her dirty work because we can't be captured or questioned.

Killing people is child's play. I can make it look like a busy street is safe to cross, or an empty pool is full of water.

Once I made a cigar cutter look like a condom. That was my best work. But Rowan says that Emma is not normal. I cannot make Emma see or hear what I want, so I must trick someone else into killing her. A more complicated task.

In the late evening someone knocks on Emma's door and the nosy neighbor pops up to peep. Through his eyes I see that it's a family in the hallway, a mother with two daughters. The teen daughter is too old for my purposes, but the younger one looks promising.

I leap into the head of the little one. I don't enjoy this perspective, looking up to see everyone. I feel like a mouse underfoot.

Emma is not at home, and the little girl, Kaya, is asking her mother why. Kaya is obviously close to Emma. Yes, perhaps this girl will do.

❦

Most people think that sleepwalking is a disorder found primarily among children. Bill has twins, and they sleepwalk nearly every night. But I know the truth, that sleepwalking is the only way ghosts can enjoy operating in a body, if only for a short time. Sleepwalking is our version of a joyride.

I spend most of my nights with Bill's twins. Their mother is useless so it's up to me to raise them right. I have taught them many useful things about the world. One night I embody Peter and use his body to speak to Paul. The next night I switch. I'd like to be with them now but I have work to do.

As Kaya sleeps under her dinosaur sheets, I bring her to a half-wakened state. She puts up no resistance. The more creative and adventurous the child, the easier they are to control. Dull kids are the most difficult.

Kaya shares a room with the older girl, who has gone to bed with her makeup on. Her mother is obviously not supervising her properly. When I worked at Child Protective Services, I would look for these signs of neglect. Never listen to what a parent tells you—always examine the child.

My own mother, normally a foul-mouthed harridan, could summon a golden tongue whenever CPS came around. Not once did they look under my long sleeves for the burns on my arms. Cretins! Why would a child wear a sweater in the middle of summer?

Kaya steps jerkily across the room. It feels so wonderful to control her body. The dark thoughts of Mother fade away.

The thing I miss most about having a body is spending time in the kitchen. I was a fabulous cook. I lead Kaya into the tiny kitchen to see what I have to work with.

I'm pleased to find raw hamburger in the refrigerator. I mix in eggs, breadcrumbs, dried onions, and my special combination of spices. No one makes meatballs like mine. Each ball is perfectly round!

As I labor in the kitchen, I suddenly realize that dawn is approaching. Hours have passed in what seemed like minutes. Kaya's clumsy little fingers, all sticky with hamburger blood, have shaped only six perfect meatballs, and never on the first try. Some of them took dozens of attempts.

Sadly, my meatballs will have to wait. The mother will be up soon, and I still need to test how far I can push Kaya without waking her up.

I put the meatballs in the refrigerator, get a butcher knife from the drawer, and head into the mother's bedroom. The knife looks huge in Kaya's tiny hands.

The big woman is snoring. *That problem would go away if you lost some weight. A lot of weight.* She obviously hasn't been cooking healthy meals for her family.

I move Kaya to the head of the bed and raise the knife over the mother's neck. The red light of the mother's clock alarm shines like blood on the gleaming blade. This is where some children will scream and wake up. But not Kaya. I like this girl.

House of Horrors

EMMA RUE

THE MANSION I'VE DISCOVERED reeks of decay. The air crawls with dust and mold and I find myself sneezing, alarmed that I'm announcing my presence to any creatures within. I inch my way through the blackness, banging my shin on some hidden obstacle. After what seems like an hour but is probably minutes, I spot a faint glow and it leads me into a kitchen where moonlight streams through a window. The vast kitchen is as big as my entire apartment. There is no running water and no electricity. The appliances look very old, perhaps from the 1950s, sturdy and unadorned. The counter is paved with slabs of marble, possibly pink, though it's hard to tell in this dim light.

There is no refrigerator, so I search through the cupboards for anything to eat or drink. All I find is a dusty bottle of wine and some homemade jerky in heat-sealed plastic. I find a corkscrew in a drawer and open the bottle. The handwritten label tells me it's a private stock Greenvale Farm chardonnay from 1927. How long does wine last in storage? I guess I'll find out.

A small sip from the bottle has me choking and spitting. It tastes like paint thinner.

The jerky is so salty that it could probably last a thousand years in storage. I've never had to chew so hard. I can feel each bite traveling all the way down to my stomach. I don't think they had heat-sealed plastic in 1927, so someone must have made this jerky more recently.

Feeling thirstier, but a little stronger, I dig through a utility closet adjacent to the kitchen. I can't tell what most of the items are, so I carry everything out into the shaft of moonlight. The only useful thing I discover is a box of long wooden matches. There may be candles somewhere in this house!

I reluctantly leave my kitchen oasis, burning a long match to light the way. I feel a moment of panic as the match winks out, but my fumbling fingers soon light another.

I catch a glimpse of something dark scurrying along a floorboard. This house has gone unattended for decades and the vermin have run amok. Perhaps I can convince them I'm their leader. Emma, Queen of Rats.

I can't see far enough in the match light to determine the size of the room I'm in now. There appears to be nothing here but cobwebs and mold. My heart leaps as I spot a treasure resting in a layer of dust along a ledge. A candelabra! I light the three stocky candles and hold them before me like a shield, venturing farther into the dark recesses of the wrecked mansion.

The ceiling suddenly disappears, stretching beyond the reach of the candlelight. I realize I'm standing in the Great Hall of Refuge d'Amoureux. Though I can't see the domed ceiling, I recognize the shape of the long dining table, easily seating thirty guests, and I see the tall windows, one of them framing the moon. Before it went to seed, the mansion must have been renovated again. That's probably when the extra floor was added. But at least this room hasn't changed.

My feet crunch on some unidentifiable debris as I cross the hall, expecting to find the grand stairs. They are right where they're supposed to be. The stairs rise to the two floors above, and a smaller staircase leads down into the basement. I'm not sure where to go from here.

I'm scared to go down into the basement. The upper floors seem safer. But for some reason I am drawn to the basement.

I take the old wooden stairs leading down. With each step, a nerve-jangling creak drifts down into the darkness.

The stench of decay grows stronger as I carefully cross the basement's concrete floor. Mountains of disintegrating cardboard boxes share space with wooden crates and a handful of old leather-bound trunks. There must be a lot of history here. I want to open all of the trunks like presents. But not now.

One of the candles sputters ominously as I press forward. The basement seems vast. I can't see its edges in the candlelight. I hear a strange noise. What is that? Dripping water?

I stumble over something. Adrenaline fires through my body as I struggle to hold onto the candelabra. I fall on my side and the candles go tumbling. I'm so graceful, like a ballerina.

The candles wink out, plunging me into darkness. Fortunately, I'm still clutching the box of matches. I feel blindly for the candles and manage to relight them, then I extend the candelabra toward the thing that I tripped over.

It's a human body, the source of the smell!

My stomach churns as I see a few shreds of leathery flesh still clinging to the skeleton. It's been here for a long time. I gasp as a rat leaps out of the rib cage and scurries into the shadows. Is this Julian's body? Or Cassandra's? I can't even tell the gender of the corpse.

I should be running away screaming! What is keeping me here?

I feel Cassandra's strength in me. She has seen many bodies, the bodies of dead soldiers and the bodies of her victims. She would not run away. So neither will I.

Swallowing my terror, I clamber to my feet and continue deeper into the dark basement. Something snags my dress. I look down, expecting to see a bony hand, but it's only an exposed nail. I free myself and continue on.

A sudden pain blurs my vision and makes my eyes water. I realize I've banged my head on a low-hanging pipe, or possibly a vent, leading from an immense rusted furnace in the corner of the basement.

Inside the furnace, I sense a presence.

A voice inside me says *run*. But my feet won't move. I feel my heart pounding in my chest. I can't breathe. Am I having a heart attack?

Drawing on Cassandra's strength, I put down the matches, move forward, and reach for the door of the huge furnace, already slightly ajar. I slowly pull it open with a trembling hand. The rusted metal shrieks as the iron door gives way.

Inside, a figure lies on the cold floor of the furnace, covered in a thin cocoon of spiderwebs. Pale spiders, hundreds of them, scuttle away from the candlelight in a sickening wave.

My hand shakes violently as I reach down and wipe cobwebs from the figure's face. His features are pinched and pale. Is he dead? Is this another body? I lean in for a closer look. Suddenly, I recognize him.

Julian!

Silverweave

Stefan Hildebrand

I realize it's dark now and I can hear the chirp of crickets. I've been meandering through the woods for hours on the way back to my car. I can't make any sense of the Summoner's death or my parents' divorce. Everything has changed for the worse.

My own father has ordered me to kill an innocent. When I was growing up, he told me that in this war of normal versus paranormal, there are no innocents. I don't agree. Emma doesn't deserve to die in a soul cage. But I can't go against my clan. No one ever has. The Ulfhednar are team players. Individual needs are sacrificed for the good of the pack. It's gotta be that way. If we lose clan cohesion, we lose this war.

One of my dad's guys shadows me a half mile back. It's the usual way of seeing someone out of our territory, but it makes me feel like I'm not trusted.

My bad mood grows as I approach the edge of the forest. I don't want to return to the city. I want to stay in these woods and be treated like family again.

My wolf speaks to me. *Hunt.*

It's a perfect night for hunting. The full moon hangs like a white platter in the sky. My wolf has been bottled up inside me for a long time. He needs this, so I invoke.

When channeling Him, my human/wolf body is able to run down and kill prey, but first I have to find it. As I jog through the woods, I see every broken twig on the forest floor. I hear the rustle of small creatures in the undergrowth. I smell animals that passed by a week ago. An Ulfhedinn's senses are actually better than a wolf's. His vargr senses meld with mine and together we are greater than the sum of our parts. I stop at a game trail to check for a scent. A white-tailed deer passed by here in the last few minutes. In all my hunts, I've never found prey so fast.

I slip quietly down the narrow trail, taking my time. I'm downwind so there's no need to rush. As I get closer, I can tell she's a doe with a fawn nearby. The doe's ears twitch as she hears me. She leaps and crashes through the woods in full retreat. White-tails are fast, but I'm faster. I might be able to run her down, but the fawn is better prey. Kill a fawn, one fawn dies. Kill a doe, and all her future fawns die.

With the moon higher now, I return to my car with the usual post-kill high. My wolf is happy. And I'm happy when He's happy.

As I prepare to release Him, I smell a foul odor. A scent that doesn't belong in the forest.

Silver.

Silver is weird. It's created only when certain stars go supernova. It has the highest electrical conductivity of any metal. In this world, energy flows freely through silver, but it has the opposite effect in the nonmaterial world. It blocks the connection between spirits and the bodies they would connect with, wreaking havoc on ghosts, demons, and the were.

KoR uses silver for everything. If they could, they'd brush their teeth with it.

I keep my wolf with me as I circle the area. It doesn't take long to spot a Knight of Rome in full silverweave combat armor, observing my car through night vision field glasses. The armor is what I smelled, a black composite material with silver threads woven in a tight diamond pattern. Over his heart is a golden laurel wreath on a field of blood. A full helm protects his head and throat, with a clear, silverglass visor covering his face. Any part of that armor can stop a bullet.

KoR knows I'm here! How did they find me? A tracker in my car?

There's no need to panic. My family lives in this area and KoR doesn't know they're were. There's nothing wrong with me coming to see them. I've got a believable cover story.

I move around to stay out of his line of sight. Suddenly, I hear a high-pitched digital shriek. Shit! The surveillance man deployed a motion sensor alarm to cover his back.

I uninvoke and move in. My wolf can't help me now. Any contact with that silverweave armor and my link with Him would break, leaving me confused. That's a bad thing in a fight. But as always, my wolf retains a small presence inside me, prepared to jump in if I need Him. They keep one paw on the ground, as my dad likes to say.

The observer turns, spotting me. A shaft of pale moonlight catches his visor. I recognize his broad bearded face. It's Rob Baxter, the senior guy on Fortunata Golde's crew. Baxter came in a few years before me. I heard he's smart, and I heard he can fight.

Baxter makes no effort to reach for his KoR-made .50-caliber gas-operated pistol loaded with pre-fragmented silver bullets. He's not stupid. At this close distance, I'd be on him before he could use it.

I make no move for my five-inch, double-edged boot knife. A knife is useless against his silverweave armor.

He acknowledges me with a curt nod. "Hildebrand."

I return his nod. "Baxter."

As I stand still, the motion alarm stops blaring. No one but Baxter has appeared. He may be alone here. I can see from his body language that he's about to attack. But why?

I suddenly realize I have deer blood on my mouth and shirt.

Baxter knows what I am. There's nothing left but to fight.

He's in a good position to win this. I'm a better fighter, but he's got armor and I don't. Armor is a huge factor. It means that strikes are off the table. I'll have to rely on joint locks and throws.

He knows I'm good so he'll probably be conservative, using kicks to keep me off him, maybe taking out a knee to start.

My fingers begin to move in odd patterns, but I still them by force of will.

No point in drawing this out any further. *Hurry to act, worry distracts.*

The motion alarm blares as I move forward in a low stance and he surges toward me, moving shockingly smooth for someone in full silverweave. He's an athletic fighter, but a mediocre tactician. He feints a punch and launches a stamp kick at the inside of my leading knee. Exactly as I expected. But can I take advantage?

I slip my leg back and trap the kick with my arm, then lash out with my shin, sweeping his supporting leg. As he falls, I take his trapped foot in both hands and twist it violently, breaking his ankle and knee. To his credit, he remains silent.

Twisting his injured leg, I flip him over on his stomach. Then I mount his back, reach over his head to grab the base of his visor, and pull his helm back until his neck snaps.

The whole fight lasts three seconds. That's about average in Ars Duellica.

I feel sick and ashamed. Baxter's not the first man I've killed, but he's the first Knight. In other circumstances, he would have given his life for me. He didn't deserve to go out this way.

Fucking Fortunata. She's behind this. She put a man on me because she's looking for dirt, something that will keep me from becoming Artufex. I wish she had come herself, even if it meant losing a fight to her.

Probably no one but Fortunata will ever know how Baxter died. If she reports it, she'll lose her knighthood for acting outside of orders and getting a man killed.

The important thing is to return to Providence and finish my Knight's Quest. I have to act as if none of this ever happened.

In the gloom of the trees behind me, I hear a faint whistle. It's my father's guy, letting me know he's there.

I don't have time to dispose of Baxter's body. The clan can do it. They have a special wood chipper for that. They call it Bone Eater.

I take a final look at my home forest and say goodbye. Who knows how long it will be until I return.

I hurry to my car. As I get inside, I smell what might be an oil leak.

As I turn the key, I realize the smell is Harrisite, a lethal plastic explosive.

Yours Eternally

EMMA RUE

I stare at Julian's body, wrapped in spider webs on the floor of the furnace. I try to speak but nothing escapes my lips.

He has a scent like rotting wood. It smells … wrong. I swallow, trying to revive my dry throat. "Julian?"

One of his eyes snaps open.

I yelp and stumble back. A candle from the candelabra tumbles to the floor and dies.

Julian's head slowly tilts back to a nearly impossible angle, both of his dark eyes now open. I see the rose-gold color slowly return to his irises as he grows more awake.

I look past his face, into his soul. The colors of his spirit flare from a spark to a fire as he awakens. It matches Cassandra's memory of him, with only a few small differences. Has he changed over the centuries?

He speaks with a slight British accent, his voice like gravel. "Cassandra?"

"Yes, Julian, but my name is Emma now." I move cautiously toward him.

A sudden anger consumes his sunken features and his voice seethes. "What took you so long??"

His fury hits me like a slap in the face. This is not the Julian I remember. I don't know what to say to him.

His cocoon of spider webs splits as he rolls over and struggles to his hands and knees.

Should I help him? I'm afraid to touch him.

He gets slowly to his feet, moving like an old man. I see two ivory fangs as he licks his cracked lips. Before I realize it, his skeletal hands have seized me. Though he looks frail, his speed is amazing and his strength incredible.

Locked in his iron grip, I feel a primal terror, like a small animal about to be eaten. My voice sounds small and shaky. "You're hurting me."

His papery fingers move across my body as if he owns it. "I need to feed."

I struggle wildly, futilely, dropping the candelabra. One of the candles remains lit on the floor.

He croaks a laugh. "Not you, my gem. You're too precious to be used in such a manner." He loosens his grip, picks up the burning candle, and hands it to me.

Relief washes over me. Suddenly I'm flooded with questions. "How did you know I was Cassandra? Did you recognize my soul? What does it look like?" *I've never been able to see my own soul, and I've always wondered.*

He holds up a hand to silence me. "I've no patience for your questions now. I need to feed. Wait in your room. It's on the second floor, to the left. You can prattle on when I return. I'll bring you food and water."

I picture the corpse outside. I'll have to walk past it again. My voice trembles as I speak. "There's a body out there."

Julian flicks his hand dismissively. "It's difficult to find housekeepers willing to clean up such messes."

"Whose body is it?"

He pushes me away, his voice sharp. "A nobody, so far as I know. I made *coppiette* of him. It's good to have on hand when I emerge from dormancy."

A feeling of dread sweeps through me. "What's coppiette?"

He growls an answer. "The Americans call it jerky."

The jerky in the heat-sealed bag! I fall to my knees, vomiting at Julian's feet. For some reason I don't want to look weak, so I quickly wipe my mouth clean and glare at him. "I may have cheated on my scholarship application, but I draw the line at cannibalism."

He laughs, a grating sound. "Go to your room and wait for me."

I blink and he disappears in front of me. I think about running far from this place. Julian is not the sweet, beautiful man that Cassandra once knew. He's a monster now. But he's a monster who can answer my questions. And I'm not leaving without answers.

The hinges squeak painfully as I force the bedroom door open. I hold up a candle and take a journey through time. The shadowy room is just as Cassandra kept it two hundred years ago!

I remember Cassandra being here, Ida helping her with her corset. Even with the thick layer of dust and the peeling wallpaper, the room is recognizable.

I go inside, looking for more candles to light. I find only one, on a hardwood writing desk. It helps to relieve the gloom.

On the vanity I find a leather-bound jewelry case. I gasp as I open it, discovering a fortune in antique jewelry: a pair of gold earrings with drops carved from some lavender stone; a silver brooch in the shape of a lyre with golden strings and turquoise inlay; and a pearl choker with an ivory disk in the front, painted with an image of Cassandra's face. I dig my hands into the jewelry, feeling its weight, soaking in the history.

What more is there to explore in this amazing room?

My wandering eyes find a four-poster bed. Beside it, a nightstand with a brass servant's bell. I lift the candle and move closer to investigate. The posts of the bed are made from a pale wood, hand-carved with flowers and bees. Is this the bed I once shared with Julian?

I peel back the rotted bed covers. The mattress seems to be in good shape. I press my hand into it. Lumpy, but not bad after 200 years. I climb onto the bed. The pillows are mostly feathers and rotted fabric. I push them onto the floor. That's when I see a parchment roll, tied with the remnants of a red ribbon. It was under one of the pillows.

My pulse quickens. Some sort of note?

I quickly remove the ribbon and gingerly unroll the stiff parchment. It crackles in my hand. The ink is faded but still legible. It's a handwritten letter from Julian!

Cassandra, my life, my world, my only love.

I miss you terribly. The moon fell from the sky when you were so wickedly taken from this world. I have no will to continue without you, but I must, in the desperate hope that one day you will remember our life together and your soul will find its way here. I pray each night for such a blessing. Until your return, I live in a world without color, without joy, like a dog lying on the grave of his master. You were everything to me, and God willing, you will be again. If you should find this letter, wake me immediately. If death has claimed me before that time, take this house into your possession, for one day my soul will return to find you. Your heartblaze ring is in the safe behind the mirror. Remember what those rings meant to us. Please do not forget me. Though battered by the storms of passing centuries, our love will endure. You must believe that.

Yours eternally, Julian.

December 1816.

My tears splatter onto the parchment. Cassandra was so blessed. How many people, in their entire lives, are lucky enough to find a love like this? I will keep this letter forever.

The Julian in the basement is not the same man who wrote this. Time has destroyed that man. Quiet sobs escape me, each releasing a wave of pain. I feel as if someone has died.

What is this heartblaze ring? I have a vague memory of wearing it, perhaps on my trip to Washington with Julian. I must find it. It's my last connection to him. I feel a sudden, powerful need to have it on my finger.

I put the letter from Julian on the vanity and examine the dust-covered mirror. The mirror swivels, but not enough to reveal the wall behind it. Then I realize the mirror can be lifted from its frame. I remove it from the vanity and set it aside.

I see the door of a rusty iron safe, set into the wall. It opens with a key. A key I don't have.

In a frenzy, I dig through the vanity, the desk, everywhere I can think to look.

No key.

I want to weep, but I am all cried out. A weariness overtakes me and I crawl back onto the bed. I lie on my stomach, head resting on my crossed arms. I find myself drawn back into Cassandra's world. I think she has something important to show me.

Papa

CYNTHIA GREENE

Kaya's mother has left to file a missing person report on Emma. I watch through Kaya's eyes as a sulking Seble remains behind to make Saturday morning breakfast for Kaya, a bowl of cereal.

Seble brings the plastic bowl to the threadbare sofa where Kaya sits, half-asleep in front of a TV that isn't turned on.

Kaya shakes her head, refusing it. And no wonder; cereal is not a healthy breakfast.

Seble frowns. "Mom says you have to eat something. I think we have eggs. You want eggs?"

Kaya doesn't answer. Frustrated, Seble takes the bowl back to the kitchen.

Seble and her mother are grossly incompetent caretakers. Neither have even noticed the perfect meatballs that Kaya sculpted during the night, and Kaya is still in her pajamas, hair a mess. It seems that no one cares. No one except me.

When I was alive, I had my way of dealing with incompetent mothers. And how did the State thank me? By locking me away in prison. This is what is wrong with our society. The little things, such as girls still being in their pajamas after 9 a.m., eventually escalate into larger problems like drugs and prostitution. Thinking about this gets me so upset! I need to focus.

Emma has apparently gone into hiding. She's left her home and her friends, making her nearly impossible to find. I have been imagining the new body Rowan has promised me. I want her to be young and blonde, with curves that inspire men to foolish acts. But I feel that body slipping away, all because of Emma. I can't bear to lose that beautiful new me.

I need a strategy, something to draw Emma back, something involving Kaya. If I can just get Emma to return, I think I can make Kaya finish the job. After all, I was able to make her hold a knife over her sleeping mother.

Kaya curls up on the sofa in her pink bunny slippers and clutches a tattered shirt to her face, her security blanket. Kids really shouldn't have those. It will be no protection against the troubles of the real world. The shirt has a faded picture of Kaya and her dad printed on the back, taken on some thrill ride. I haven't seen him anywhere. He probably abandoned his family. Typical man.

I have an idea, but first I'll need to deal with Seble, who has just found the meatballs and is quite puzzled by the discovery. Seble's phone beeps as she gets a text message.

I hop into her head as she reads the junk text, something about tires. Earlier this morning, she was talking to her mother about some boy, Philip. Philip this and Philip that. So I think this text should be from Philip. I can't change what the phone actually shows, but I can change what Seble *sees* when she reads it.

One minute later, an outraged Seble marches to her room, calling a friend to complain that Philip thinks she's "underinflated."

Perfect. Kaya is alone now.

Inside Kaya's head, I imagine her father's whispering voice. I have no idea what he sounds like, but hopefully I can fool a five-year-old. "Kaya? It's Daddy."

She sits up, groggy, and looks around the room. "Papa?"

This is the difference between an adult and a child. An adult would be running by now. "Yes, Kaya, it's Papa. Can you see my picture on the shirt?"

She unfolds the shirt and runs her fingers over the worn and cracked image. "Where are you?"

Probably in the arms of a woman twenty years younger than your mother. "I'm here, Kaya. I came to talk to you about your friend Emma. I'm worried about her."

"Emma ran away."

"I know, Kaya. I'm sorry. But if you help me, we can get her back. Will you help Papa?"

"Yes! I want to help!"

"If Emma calls, I want you to talk to her. Tell her that you're very sad and you can't sleep until she comes home. Do you understand?"

"Yes. I'm so sad."

"Okay, so let's practice. 'Ring ring. Hello, Kaya, this is Emma.' So now what do you say to Emma?"

"Papa wants you to come home so I can sleep."

"No, Kaya, don't say anything about Papa. *You* want Emma to come home because *you're* sad and *you* want to sleep."

Seble suddenly looms over Kaya, her face full of angry tears. "Stop yammering. I'm trying to talk on the phone!"

Kaya waves her hands in excitement. "Papa's here."

Seble shakes her head in exasperation. "Don't be stupid. You know he's dead."

Oops, that's a surprise. Though I can get inside someone's head and see through their eyes, I can't know what they are thinking or access their memories. This would be so much easier if I could.

Kaya's voice screeches. "Papa's not dead!" She holds up the shirt as proof.

Seble snatches the shirt from her sister's hand. "I'm sick of seeing this rag. Why do you keep it? Your dad was a drunk loser, Kaya. He ran over two people and killed himself. And your mom got hooked on drugs!"

Seble shreds the paper-thin fabric in her hands.

Kaya shrieks. "Stop it!" She jerks the torn shirt from Seble's hands and runs into her mother's bedroom, locking the door behind her.

Seble pounds on the outside of the door. "Unlock it or I'll call Mom!"

Kaya stands on a chair covered with clothing and opens the bedroom window.

This is getting out of hand. Time for Papa to intervene. I try to sound calming. "Kaya, honey, close the window."

"Shut your stupid face. I hate you!" She tosses the torn shirt onto the floor and crawls out the window into what appears to be a rat-infested alley littered with broken glass.

What a display of poor judgment. This is what happens when a child lacks good role models.

BLOODMATES

CASSANDRA CROSS

1776

EMMA'S PAST LIFE

SOME INTRIGUE IS AFOOT. Julian has taken me into town on a rare daylight trip. To protect our eyes, we both wear our Venetian spectacles with round rims and green-tinted glass. Our spectacles are a spectacle! It's not wise to attract such attention, but Julian secretly enjoys it.

He takes my white-gloved hand and leads me toward a crowd gathering before Newport's red brick State Building. Despite the heat, I wear my blue silk winter dress with the long sleeves. The hungry summer sun chews through it, licking at the pale skin beneath. Julian told me that in ancient times, the sun could burn the Transcendent to ash. But those who were vulnerable to that curse died centuries ago. We can walk the earth in daylight now, though it's still quite uncomfortable.

A puffing, red-faced major in the Continental Army tries

to read aloud some sort of document, but his words are lost in the din of the babbling crowd. A young lad with a giddy smile darts about, handing out copies of the document to the gentlemen present, including Julian. The title at the top reads: *The Declaration of Independence.*

The major hits his stride and begins to outshout the sweating crowd. "We hold these truths to be self-evident, that all men are created equal, that they are endowed by their Creator with certain unalienable Rights, that among these are Life, Liberty and the pursuit of Happiness."

A deafening cheer erupts from the crowd. I feel a sudden thrill. What bold words! But what is their meaning? What of slaves? Are they equal? Are they not men? And more troubling, what of women? Why didn't they write "all *people* are created equal?"

The major speaks for several more minutes before concluding to raucous applause. This document is largely a prolonged poke in the eye of Great Britain. Of course, the war has been raging for a year now, and those who rebelled don't need a piece of paper to explain why. Nonetheless, it's brilliantly worded and will no doubt have tremendous propaganda value. Truly, this feels like a historic moment.

As Julian and I leave the gathering, he waves his copy of the document. "I wanted you to witness this event." He guides me into the carriage with a barely suppressed grin of delight. I sense that his little intrigue is not yet played out. As he sits across from me, the carriage jostles and the State House disappears from view. He puts down the document and takes both of my hands in his. "Do you enjoy being married to me?"

I nod. *What is his game?*

He's smiling, but beneath his expression I see that he is nervous. It reminds me of when he proposed, the day after I finally managed to divorce Tom. That was such a scandal. I was so shaken from the emotional and legal fight that I didn't see Julian's proposal coming. He mistook my confusion for displeasure. He thought I would say no.

Julian continues, his voice dropping to a whisper, "I thought perhaps we could declare our own independence."

I suddenly understand his game. Julian St. Fleur, my husband, my Maker, the one true love of my life, wishes for us to become bloodmates. This is a Transcendent relationship more sacred than marriage, a step normally taken decades into a relationship, if ever, and we have been together for less than a year. We have only just received our invitation to join the League of Brush and Quill, our entrée into polite Transcendent society. Will this create a scandal? If so, I really don't care. I want Julian. I want him in any way, in every way possible. I give him my smile. *"Bonne idée."*

His sudden embrace shakes the carriage and bruises my arms.

Happy tears flood my eyes as I see his joy. But I must speak my mind. "I have but one condition."

I take off my spectacles and he does the same. He peers deep into my eyes, into my soul. "Anything, my love, anything you desire."

As midnight approaches, Julian leans over my candlelit writing desk to read the revision I have made to our copy of the Declaration of Independence. Where it once read…

We hold these truths to be self-evident, that all men are created equal…

It now reads…

We hold these truths to be self-evident, that all people are created equal…

I look into his eyes, my voice serious. "I won't be an inferior in this relationship."

He nods solemnly as I sign the bottom of the document. I hand him the quill and he does the same. "I think that you should be leading this revolution, my love."

I run my hands across the stiff paper. I will treasure this document always.

Julian kneels before me and produces a dark wooden ring box with a brocaded face. I open it and discover a treasure resting on a cushion of black velvet, a heartblaze ring, traditionally worn by bloodmates. I can't pull my eyes away from it. The burgundy gem is set in a frame of gold petals, forming a beautiful and dangerous rose. Blood-bright meteors flash from deep within the stone as its facets catch the light. The sturdy band has been carved away to reveal a twisted circle of rose-gold thorns. It's not just a ring, it's a stunning piece of Gothic art.

Julian is already wearing a twin of the same ring.

"Cassandra Cross, you are my northern star, guiding me true when I am lost. Through your eyes I see the wonders of a world I never knew. The life we share is a treasure beyond measure, but I beg you for more. Grant me a hundred lives, a thousand lives together. I beseech you, be my bloodmate and let our souls come together in the light of the eternal moon."

Tears cloud my eyes and I feel my heart flutter. My voice has fled. All I can do is nod my assent.

Smiling with profound joy, he slips the ring onto the fourth finger of my right hand.

I manage two choked words as we embrace. "It's lovely."

"The ring was crafted by Minos, Master Jeweler of the Black Rose Society. His creations have adorned emperors. The gem is blazestone, rather dark to mortal eyes but rippling blood-red to our own. Your stone will absorb a fraction of my essence, and mine will claim a piece of yours. Once it's done, when you look upon it, you will see the state of my soul, however far away I am. You will know when I am happy or sad, and you will know when I need you most."

"What a remarkable thing! When will we perform the ceremony?"

He smiles slyly. "Remove your garments and meet me on the roof. They're waiting for us."

The wheels are already in motion? My, that was remarkably confident of him. What if I had said no? But that's what I love about him. He knows my heart. "All of my clothes?" He nods and starts to leave. A worry stabs me. "Wait, what about Angelo? Will he try to disrupt the ceremony?"

Angelo Weis was Julian's Maker, a horrible creature who created him through carelessness. Julian was born a blood child, an accident. Angelo could barely be troubled to teach Julian the secrets of Transcendency. When Julian expressed an interest in me, Angelo became envious, wanting me for his own. But I belong to Julian St. Fleur.

Julian stops at the door, whispering a reassurance. "Have no fear, my love. He's in the Indies, playing the privateer."

I nod. With any luck, a royal cannonball will separate his head from his body.

Julian leaves. Before I undress, I have one last thing to do. I find a particular carved bee on one of my wooden bedposts. As I twist the bee, a hidden nook opens. I take a key from inside and use it to open the safe behind my mirror. I roll up my signed document and lock it away.

The time has come.

Completely nude, I ascend the narrow wooden stairs leading to the roof of Refuge d'Amoureux. I tremble with nervous excitement. What awaits me? I have no idea how this ceremony is performed. What if I make some hideous faux pas?

I slip through a tiny door, emerging under a blanket of stars and the moon's silver platter.

Julian has somehow brought our bed to the roof. The beautiful mahogany four-poster bed was built by John Goddard, a local craftsman of great renown. Julian and I each have our own rooms and our own beds; we use our own when the other is away. But when we're together we use the communal room and the communal bed made by Goddard. How on earth did Julian get it through that tiny door?

Julian stands nude at the foot of the bed. I admire the lean curves of his muscles. I know every detail of that remarkable body; every inch of it is drawn on the map of my heart.

Beside him stand two figures in black velvet robes. I recognize them from the Society: Lorance Sparkes, Governor of the New England Domain, and Hope Fenwick, Speaker for the Town of Newport. Both are respected figures in the Transcendent hierarchy. But I feel a flush of anger that Julian's charms are exposed to Hope's glittering dark eyes. Will she still be here when it comes time to use the bed? If she is, I will surely tear her eyes out.

I join Julian, taking his hand in mine. My nervousness fades at his touch, as it always does.

He whispers softly to me. "Tonight, my love, Newport does not exist. There is only Refuge d'Amoureux."

I look out over the town in astonishment. Newport lies dark. Not so much as a candle in sight. No wonder the stars are so bright. How on earth has Julian arranged this?

He flashes a knowing smile as the governor steps before us, hands hidden in his dark robe, his jutting chin catching the starlight. Lorance is a great man, a Society Noble, a soulreader without peer. Can he read the record of my sins? I think back on Tom's face when I asked him for the divorce, those hot tears on his cheeks.

The governor speaks. I've never heard him so cheerful. "Julian and Cassandra, it is my great pleasure to join you together, blood and soul. Once joined, you cannot be separated, so do not make this vow in haste. Julian St. Fleur, are you certain you wish to embark on this journey, a journey without end?"

Julian's voice radiates confidence, filling me with strength. "I am certain."

The governor turns to me. "Cassandra St. Fleur, are you certain you wish to embark on this journey, a journey without end?"

"I am certain."

"Then so it shall be. The Black Rose Society gladly recognizes this blood union. May fate bind you together for eternity."

I turn to kiss Julian, lost for a moment in the wonder of his soft lips.

Turning back, I see that Lorance and Hope have stepped into Velox and left us alone here in Mortalos.

Julian lies down on the bed. The Transcendent can couple as humans do, but it's rarely as satisfying as *conventus,* a mutual bite in which our bodies and souls merge together while our mouths release a narcotic, called bliss, into the blood of the other. Nothing else can compare. Conventus, also known as the blood embrace, can last for hours.

Tonight, under the cold light of the stars, I will share this bed with the man I love, the man I will love forever.

Julian gently pulls me down to him. His mouth finds my neck and I feel him claim a portion of my blood and soul. I see my essence enter his heartblaze ring, illuminating the burgundy stone with soul-light.

I drink from Julian and soon a part of his soul lives within my ring. He whispers to me in the True Tongue, a rapid, nearly silent whisper that only the Transcendent can understand. He speaks of his love for me and the future we will have together. He promises to nurture and cherish me in this life and the next. He swears that he will never raise a hand or speak a harsh word against me.

I know he means every word. But will his promises stand the test of time? Will he feel the same way in a hundred years, or two hundred? Who can say? The time will pass quickly enough, and eventually I will know.

Rogue Stars

Emma Rue

THE PRESENT

I wake and crawl from the bed to look out the window of Cassandra's room. It looks to be about noon! I hadn't meant to sleep this long. For a half second I worry that I'm missing class. Then I remember that I've been expelled and that I need to find a second job to supplement my income at the library. Or perhaps Melita can convince them to extend my hours.

Melita! I have to find a phone and call her. I disappeared from the hospital without telling her. She must be worried sick. I'm such a wonderful friend. I bet she wishes she had two more just like me.

But first I have to open that hidden safe where Cassandra keeps her most precious things. Remembering my dream of her, I find the carved bee on the bedpost. It turns, revealing the nook with the small key to the safe inside!

I begin to worry as I remove the dusty mirror and unlock

the hidden safe, which opens with surprising ease. What if Julian has taken Cassandra's belongings?

To my great relief, I see the heartblaze ring and the Declaration of Independence inside the safe. I pick up the beautiful ring. It feels strangely heavy in my hand. Is it the weight of Julian's soul?

I slide the ring onto my finger. A perfect fit. I see faint colors slowly drifting within the blazestone, not nearly as strong as they were in Cassandra's memories. Either Cassandra's vision was much better than mine, or Julian's feelings for me have faded.

As I begin to close the door of the safe, I notice something behind the Declaration, a knife made of green metal with emeralds set in the handle. I pick it up. It feels alive and dangerous, and I see the faint traces of a soul. I recognize the dagger from Cassandra's memory. Síndóm.

Downstairs I hear a door closing. I quickly put Síndóm back in the safe, lock it, and rush to return the key to its hiding place in the bedpost.

Julian enters, dressed in a slim-fitting, midnight-blue three-piece suit with a narrow purple tie. Bad boy runway model meets high-powered CEO. His pale skin is slightly flushed, his butterscotch hair flowing behind him. He looks just like the Julian from Cassandra's memories. An Adonis carved in flesh.

I open my mouth to speak, but nothing comes out.

He glides over to me, his arms tightening around my body like steel cables. Looking into his soul, I see desire, anger, and other things too complex to fathom.

Up close, his smell is … masculine, intoxicating. Images flash through my mind. Gold leaves in autumn. A red sunset over a smoky mountain. My arms and legs weaken, and I slump in his arms. I have a sudden, desperate need to be … consumed … by him.

His deft fingers slowly, teasingly undo each button of my dress.

I want him to hurry.

As I stare at him, eyes wide with anticipation, I see his beautiful, perfect smile. But it's a self-satisfied smile. He sees this as a domination, a victory.

With a monumental exercise of will, I turn away from him and whisper, "No."

He looks stunned and angry. But there's also a hint of grudging respect. He speaks through tight lips. "Why so reluctant, Cassandra?"

"I'm Emma, Julian, not Cassandra. Can you please say my name, just once? *Emma.*"

"Enough. You're boring me!"

He turns to leave. I suddenly fear that I will never see him again, never have my questions answered. "Wait! I'm sorry. Please stay. I have a question."

He returns with a smirk, satisfied that I have begged him to stay, as he knew I would.

I ask him the question most on my mind. "Can you tell me what happened to Cassandra?"

A dark cloud passes over his face. "She was assassinated by

the Knights of Rome, a group that hunts the Transcendent."

No wonder he's so bitter. Who are these Knights of Rome? "That must have been hard to deal with."

He waves off my comment. I see that he's not wearing his heartblaze ring. His manner becomes businesslike. "You will remain in this room. I'll bring you a chamber pot as well as food and water as you need it."

Chamber pot! "I'm not your prisoner, Julian."

"It seems that you are."

I hold up the finger with the ring. "Have you forgotten your vow?"

"Ah, the heartblaze ring. I sold mine years ago, when I gave up hope of a reunion. You should have returned sooner."

He's hurting me to cover his pain. "Julian, do you remember the night you became bloodmates with Cassandra?"

"No."

Liar. "Do you remember why you fell in love with her?"

His haunted eyes look into the past. His voice grows softer. "Stop."

He wants to talk about it. "Why was she so special?"

A faint smile finds his lips. "She ... you, have an old soul. Ancient, in fact. As we experience each incarnation, the colors become more vibrant, more complex. Your soul is breathtaking to behold, an untamed whirlwind of wildflowers and rogue stars. Beauty of the flesh is common, but beauty of the spirit is rare. All Transcendent know of Cassandra Cross. And all desire you."

I feel dizzy with sudden joy. That is *my* soul he's talking about! I matter in the world. There is more to me than this disaster I call my life.

Julian's voice grows hard again. "But they cannot have you. You are mine, body and soul. When next I visit your chamber, you will hold your tongue and yield up your treasures." He leaves, slamming the door behind him. Was that a piece of parchment I saw in his hand?

A sick feeling washes over me. I rush over to the vanity where I left Julian's letter.

It's gone! The bastard took it. He stole my only connection to the kind, loving Julian that Cassandra adored. Did he steal it because it shows his vulnerability? Or is it because those words were meant for Cassandra, not me? Maybe he just wants to hold it over me, to use it as a tool of control. I won't give him the satisfaction of begging for it.

I brush away tears. It's time to get out of here and tell Melita that I'm okay. I reopen the safe to collect Síndóm and the Declaration. I stow them in one of Cassandra's odd, basket-shaped purses covered with delicate embroidered flowers.

The old window takes enormous effort to open. I fear the awful grating sound will bring Julian back into the room. Heart pumping, I ease out onto the second-story ledge. If I try to jump from here, I will break my legs.

From here I can see the tomb at the back of the house, overgrown by weeds and vines. In the daylight, the stone angels look different. The vines have parted to reveal their sad, pitted faces, drawing me toward them. Is Cassandra's body in that crypt?

I sense someone behind me and turn back to the open

window. I see Julian's furious face, eyes squinting in the sunlight. I have the feeling he's about to push me off the ledge. I reach into the basket, taking Síndóm in my shaking hand and waving it at him. "Stay back!"

He steps away from the window, speaking through clenched teeth. "That … is not … a toy."

He's really afraid of the knife! Why? Does it kill vampires? I don't want to hurt him, but if I surrender, what will he do to me? I picture myself chained inside the empty furnace, those pale spiders weaving me in their webs.

I look at the ground below. It's a tangle of thorny brown brambles, thick enough to shred my skin but not enough to cushion my fall. Blood rushes in my ears as panic explodes inside me.

The world spins around me as I lose my balance and tumble awkwardly off the moss-covered second-floor ledge.

Ant Map

STEFAN HILDEBRAND

As my car engine starts, I curse myself for not checking out the "oil" smell. An amateur mistake. Maybe I'm not cut out to be a Knight. I wonder if the plastic explosive will leave any pieces big enough for my family to recognize.

Why am I still alive?

Invoking my wolf, I burst from the car and roll clear. Still no explosion. Maybe the device has a wireless detonator and Baxter isn't alive to push the button.

I uninvoke and walk back to search Baxter's broken body. I find the transmitter. Baxter hadn't been running surveillance; his mission was a straight-up assassination. He was using an encoded, wireless detonator, safer to rig than a pressure sensor and less likely to blow up the wrong guy. He planted the bomb while I was in the woods and planned to push the button when I got back inside my car. Lucky thing I killed him first.

I return to the car and find the explosive lurking under the seat. Baxter was working fast here, no anti-tampering devices. I carefully remove the receiver.

Fortunata just raised this feud to a whole new level. A year ago she set the all-time high score on the Ars Duellica final, and then this year I beat her score by a point. She thinks I cheated, accused me of colluding with someone who had already taken the test. That's bullshit, of course, but she couldn't be talked out of it. And now that I'm on track to become Artufex, she wants me dead. The thing is, even with me out of the way, she'll never get a job like that. She's not a people person. I once told her that and she broke my nose.

As I reach the outskirts of Providence, I check the sky out the front windshield. Dawn's almost here. In the southeast, Venus shines like an oncoming jetliner.

I need to find Emma. But I also need to watch my back. I knew Fortunata was bold, but I didn't know she was so reckless. She might decide to make another attempt on my life. I realize now that my original plan—to ignore her—was stupid. I have to stop her, or at least slow her down, and I have to do it soon.

But first I have to get out of this bloodstained shirt and grab Emma. It's too risky to go to the apartment that KoR set up for me near the college. I have a clean sweatshirt in my gym locker. I can get washed up there.

Emma's building manager, a bitchy dude, isn't happy to see me so early in the morning. But I flash my "FBI" badge and he takes me to her apartment. Most KoR field agents carry FBI credentials. It's helpful for dealing with local police. And if anyone runs the badge numbers, they actually check out. KoR has lots of friends with the Feds. We solve the problems they can't handle. "We"? Where did that come from? I'm not one of them.

Emma doesn't answer when I knock, so the manager reluctantly lets me in. He wants to hover and I have to order him out to get some privacy. Emma has a shitty apartment in an even shittier neighborhood. It looks like a bomb shelter, but instead of sandbags stacked against the walls, she has books.

The kitchen smells like a drug lab. It looks like she's making her own paper. There's no food in the fridge, just a half-empty bottle of wine. Isn't she too young to buy alcohol?

Suddenly, I feel a familiar warmth in the back of my head. My wolf? I didn't invoke Him.

With a chill, I realize it isn't my wolf. I violently push the spirit away. Is it a ghost, a demon? Something is definitely haunting this place. A normal human would have no idea when they had a rider, but the were do this for a living.

I whisper a message to the foiled spirit. "Nice try."

I exit the kitchen and check out the bedroom, where I find Emma's mobile phone, a really old model. She told me once she never carries it. Why? Is she afraid of being tracked? I check the phone and find a couple of worried messages from someone named Melita. Emma apparently left without telling her friends. What was she running from? Me?

I check her phone log and find that her last outgoing call was made yesterday afternoon. I call the number and reach a recording for the Preservation Society, the people who run the Newport mansions. Has Emma actually gone to Newport, KoR's command center for the entire New England region? How ironic. She'd be running straight into the jaws of the lion that's chasing her.

Hundreds of years ago, Newport was a lair for pirates and vampires. KoR set up shop there to bring back law and order. Now the biggest worry the city has is who forgot to pay the docking fees for their yacht. Emma would stand out there like a neon sign.

If Emma went to Newport, why? And why didn't she do a better job of hiding her trail? She isn't acting like someone who's on the run. She's acting like someone who's on the hunt.

This girl just gets more and more interesting. I look around her bedroom. There isn't much here, just a bed and a couple dozen boxes of books. I see something hanging on the wall and step closer. It's an oversized page from some Shakespeare play, pressed behind glass. The yellowing paper and old-fashioned font make me wonder if it's an original.

Damn, why is KoR so scared of Emma? She's not exactly supervillain material. *Library Girl. She'll shush your ass!*

I invoke my wolf and push my nose into her pillow, memorizing her scent for the hunt ahead. She smells like vanilla and strawberries. Nice.

As I wait alone outside the Preceptor's office, I try to calm my nerves. Before I turn Newport upside down looking for Emma, I need to deal with Fortunata. She'll be expecting me to fight her with field tactics and Ars Duellica, so the plan is to do the unexpected, to fight her with bureaucracy. The first step is making this appointment with the Preceptor. I hope it doesn't blow up in my face.

There is nothing here to look at or read. Just three wooden chairs in a small dark room. Light shines from under the Preceptor's door, occasionally broken by a moving shadow. Level Black gives me the creeps. It looks like a high-tech dungeon and the air is thick and hard to breathe. I still my twitching fingers and bite off half a roll of antacids.

The Preceptor's door swings open and Fortunata Golde walks out. Shit! The bitch anticipated my move and got here one step ahead of me. I feel a trap about to be sprung. She sits beside me, smiling with her mouthful of pink gums and hacksaw teeth, eager to speak. "The Preceptor is *not* happy. She sent me out so she could make a phone call."

Fortunata is goading me, hoping I'll beg for information. So I remain silent.

Eyes twinkling, she whispers to me, "How was Baxter? Did he even give you a fight?"

I want to smash her stupid face. I want to make her tell me why she's here, what she said to the Preceptor. But this is one of those moments where it's best to keep my mouth closed. Hunting teaches that discipline. I think of the forest, and it calms me.

The Preceptor's stern attendant opens the door and ushers us both inside. I've actually never been in Preceptor Stockhausen's office. It's warm in here. A map of the U.S. covers an entire wall. It shows the locations of all the KoR field offices and paranormal hotspots. The lines of the map are moving. I look closer and realize the whole thing is some kind of giant ant farm.

The attendant leaves and the grim-faced Preceptor sits behind a glass desk. Her harsh blue eyes direct us to the chairs across from her. Fortunata sits beside me, now hiding her smile.

Stockhausen taps her fingernails against the glass as she looks at me solemnly. "Lady Golde has informed me that Baxter is missing. Do you know anything about that?"

So Fortunata is setting me up for Baxter's death. How's she going to do that without implicating herself? "No ma'am. I don't know anything about Baxter. That's not why I came here."

Stockhausen frowns. "So you didn't call on Baxter for help on your quest?"

Smart lie, Fortunata. "No ma'am, I did not. My instructions were to do it solo."

Stockhausen squints, her eyes shifting back and forth between me and Fortunata.

Fortunata is doing her best to look confused. "That's what Baxter told me. Why would he lie about it?"

Stockhausen crosses her arms, glaring at me. "Why, indeed?"

A smirk curls the corners of Fortunata's mouth.

This is going south. Time to play my ace in the hole. I reach into my pocket, pull out a small black receiver, and place it on top of the desk. "Someone just tried to kill me. The bomb's still in my car if you want to get a forensics team in there. Harrisite with a wireless detonator. One of ours, actually." *It wasn't, of course. Fortunata would never leave KoR fingerprints, so I switched the receiver to one of ours.*

Fortunata's smirk disappears. I see worry lines on her forehead. Good, your turn to squirm.

The Preceptor examines the receiver. Her face grows increasingly troubled. "There will be a full investigation. I find it difficult to believe that this bomb and Baxter's disappearance are not related."

Fortunata's mouth opens but nothing comes out. I know the feeling.

It's time to get the hell out of here. "Ma'am, if you could have another car assigned to me, I need to be on my way. My target's on the run, and I don't want to disappoint you and Commander Amedeo."

Her face darkens at the mention of the National Commander's name. However he got mixed up in this, she isn't happy about it. The Preceptor nods, almost imperceptibly, and I'm on my feet, headed for the exit.

"Wait a moment, Squire Hildebrand. There is one other matter."

I turn to see Fortunata smiling. Shit. I was almost out the door.

Stockhausen's voice drops low and cold. The ants in the map seem to stop moving. "We checked your phone tracking data. Instead of beginning your mission as instructed, you drove to your home in Vermont. I want to know why."

She's looking at me like I'm one of those little ants crawling in her map. I wonder if she squashes them for fun.

Fate of the Maker

Emma Rue

Apparently, of all my options, falling headfirst off the ledge was the best possible choice. As I plummet to what is likely a painful death, I see Síndóm fall into the brambles, followed by Cassandra's purse with her copy of the Declaration of Independence jutting out the opening. I feel sick with terror. Why haven't I hit the ground?

I look up and see Julian holding me casually by the ankles. My dress is up around my waist with my panties on full display. Note to self: Next time you fall to your death, wear pants.

Julian sounds unworried. "I see you haven't lost your penchant for theatrics." He gathers me back through the window, taking care not to scrape me against the splintery wall or the cracked window frame. He's amazingly strong and graceful. His scent overwhelms me. As I take my feet I begin to droop toward him, wondering why I was so afraid of him before.

Vaguely, I'm aware of someone knocking downstairs. Julian sets me on the bed and steps toward the dusty vanity. I can think more clearly now that he isn't next to me. My voice comes out weak. "Thanks for catching me."

The spell he cast over me begins to fade and my fear of him returns. Who is downstairs? Would Julian dare to hurt me when there are witnesses about? Perhaps I should scream for help. Would Julian kill the witnesses? I don't have any good choices here.

The knocking grows louder. Julian sighs. "That would be the telephone company here to restore service. When I am not dormant, I summon them frequently. These devices tend to break down around our kind. I also have people coming for the electricity and water tomorrow. Afterward, you can dispense with the chamber pot."

He puts the mirror back into the frame. As he stares at his image, his features begin to change. He winces, stretching his jaw from side to side. It looks like he's in pain.

He's making my rattled nerves even worse. "What are you doing?"

"Maintaining ownership of this estate is not a trivial task. I emerge from dormancy every five years to attend to business and learn the state of the world. Over the decades, the property must appear to be passed down to relatives. The current *owner* is Richard Sinclair. In all matters of caretaking I must appear as he."

"How are you doing that to your face?"

"You really don't remember? You've done it yourself from time to time, though in my opinion, nothing compares to your original face."

I feel my frustration growing. "You still haven't answered my question." My voice sounds sharper than I intended. Oddly, that seems to lighten his mood.

"It's called metamorphosis. We can transform our bodies, mostly in small ways, though a few who have it as a greater power can morph into animals."

I feel sick as he uses his hands to move his nose a little higher on his face, accompanied by a popping sound. The mirror tilts, seemingly on its own, so that Julian can get a better view. I remember this from Cassandra. She called it a third hand.

Julian takes one last look at his new face. Richard Sinclair is an older man with thinning red hair. I don't like Richard. He looks creepy. The transformation is unnerving. I gasp as I look at his soul and see even that has changed.

Julian turns toward me. "Remain in your room. Don't create a disturbance while they're here."

I have so many questions for Julian. Now is the time to ask, while they're fixing the phones. I know Julian wants my body, but he won't attack me while other people are here. Or will he? I speak to him, hoping to strike a bargain. "I won't make a scene while they're here. But I won't be a prisoner in this room, and you need to answer some questions."

Julian smirks and turns away. He steps into the shadows behind the vanity and disappears. A moment later I hear him talking with the phone technicians downstairs. I remember Cassandra walking through a kind of shadow world she called Velox. She was able to get from Newport to Washington in a very short time. What a remarkable power!

I know I'm taking a risk, but I'll ask my questions of Julian and then leave with the technicians when they go. Julian can't risk hurting them. The phone company knows they're here. If Julian does anything to bring the police down on him, he will lose this lair he has kept for the last two hundred years.

I descend the stairs and enter the ruins of the Great Hall. Daylight streams through the tall, dirty windows, their Chinese silk curtains long since fallen into dusty shreds. This room is a withered husk of what I saw in my Cassandra dreams.

For a moment, I imagine myself living here with Julian and renovating Refuge d'Amoureux. I could be the queen of my own fairy-tale castle, complete with its own resident monster.

I feel faint. I need to eat something. But will I be able to keep it down? The memory of that human jerky makes me want to dry-heave.

I spot a painting with a broken frame lying on the debris-strewn floor. I pick it up and blow off the dust. It's Julian's painting of Cassandra's soul. It appears to be unimpressive puffs of pastel colors, like something painted by a child. Unlike Cassandra, I can only see a hint of the blaze paints that bring it to life.

As I prop the painting against the wall, I notice another frame hanging precariously from one nail on the wall. I rescue it and blow off the dust. The painting depicts a darkly handsome man in his midthirties: gray eyes, lean features, and a black goatee. He looks somehow … familiar.

Out in the foyer, I hear Julian talking to the technicians. I carry the painting out to him and hold it up. I find it hard to look at "Richard's" unpleasant face. I point to the haunting, beautiful man in the painting. "Who is he?"

Julian frowns, takes me by the arm, and hauls me back into the Great Hall. "Do not touch the paintings."

I put some steel in my voice. "Again, you didn't answer my question. Who is he?"

Julian lowers his voice so the technicians can't hear. "My Maker, Angelo. You knew him once. He was … quite taken … with you."

"What happened to him?"

Julian stares at me for the longest time, trying to come to a decision. He tears the painting from my hand and places it carefully against the wall. Then he pulls me over to the window and points to the tomb behind the house. "He's in there."

I suddenly realize that Angelo is still alive. When I first arrived, I felt his presence in that tomb, which raises even more questions. "Why doesn't he come out?"

Angry, Julian pulls me deeper into the mansion, his voice so low I can barely hear him. "Angelo was in love with you. I'm surprised you don't remember. As my Maker, he felt he had the stronger claim. But you chose me. He never fully accepted that. When you died, his obsession grew and he developed plans to find you in your next incarnation. I could not make him let go. And so he sealed his fate. I had no choice but to imprison him. He's been trapped in that tomb for nearly two hundred years, lying in a dormant state. Every decade or so I throw in someone for him to eat. Even dormant, he needs to feed occasionally in order to survive."

My head reels. A second monster at Refuge d'Amoureux! Is it wrong that I feel sorry for him? "Two hundred years in a tomb? That's incredibly cruel. It would have been more merciful to kill him."

Julian's mouth forms a hard line. On Richard's face, it looks hideous. "Have you remembered nothing? We are the Transcendent, the Makers of civilization. Murder of our own people is an appalling crime. And freeing him was not a possibility. If I had, it would have been he who met you here upon your return. Believe me when I say you would not have wanted that. I am a lamb to his lion."

A monster worse than Julian? Hard to believe.

The technicians, finished with their work, enter the Great Hall and tell us that the phones are working. I need to call Melita! I hurry into the foyer, Julian shadowing me, the technicians following us. I grab the phone and dial. I feel Julian step close behind me, his scent overpowering me, making my head reel.

I find myself staring at the phone. I must have already hung up. I have a vague recollection of talking to Melita, of her being really pissed. I feel dizzy. Hunger and thirst have taken their toll. I look around for the phone technicians, but find only Julian, no longer in the guise of Richard, draped casually across a moth-eaten chair in the foyer. He's wearing a predatory smile, and I suddenly realize why. The technicians have left. I'm alone with him.

"How is your friend, Melita?"

"I can't remember. What did you do?"

"Nothing, my gem, you just need to eat something."

I close my eyes and try to concentrate. I remember snatches of conversation, something about Kaya. "Kaya got on the phone with me. She was crying. She had tried to run away."

Julian waves his hand dismissively.

"Kaya can't sleep until she sees me again. I'm supposed to come back and give her a big hug."

Julian frowns. Perhaps I've remembered more than he intended. I'm painfully aware of how vulnerable I am to him right now. I could make a run for the door, but he'd slip into Velox and get there ahead of me. He knows he has me. Smug bastard. Maybe I can compromise with him. "I need to go home, just for a little while, to check in on Kaya. Then I'll come back."

I feel his third hand caressing my hip. "Nonsense, you'll remain here." He rises gracefully from the chair.

I freeze like a deer in the headlights as he approaches. As I look into his soul, I see a Julian like nothing in Cassandra's memories. He is bitter and hungry.

He lifts me in his arms. I go limp as I breathe his intoxicating pheromones. The smell seeps into my bones, lulling me into a blissful stupor. I see foam on dark ocean waves, a burning forest, a white avalanche cascading down an alpine peak.

I realize he has carried me into the Great Hall. He throws me onto the long table but I don't feel the pain. *Take me.*

The room begins to spin as he lifts my dress. I watch the gilded moon and stars on the domed ceiling as they fade into darkness.

Iron Eagle

Cassandra Cross

1816

EMMA'S PAST LIFE

As our coach lurches across the fetid backstreets of Philadelphia, I grow increasingly angry with Julian. Yesterday he missed our fortieth anniversary as bloodmates. It was the first anniversary he has missed, and he still hasn't realized his mistake. Can he not see that he has wounded me? I'm in no mood for an outing today, especially this fool's errand for Angelo.

I have not seen Angelo since my Transcendence—Julian endeavors to keep us apart—but I have seen Angelo's handiwork, the way he manipulates Julian. I can no longer hold my tongue. "If your Maker thought this trip so important, he could have bloody well come himself."

Julian casts his most endearing smile. And damn if it still doesn't work. "Peace, my love, he's in London on business. Our business, actually."

I feign disinterest but Julian continues, "The war devastated our economy. If he hadn't seen it coming and moved our investments overseas, we'd be living in a log cabin. Think what you will of him, but he's a keen observer and shrewd investor."

"Pah." Through my tinted spectacles, I gaze out the window of the carriage and watch the boats on the Delaware. On a waterfront dock they've towed a swollen whale in for butcher. The ghastly odor, like rotting corpses floating in human sewage, assaults my nose.

Julian reads my thoughts. "We'll be there soon, and it will smell of ink, not offal."

Ink? He's trying to pique my curiosity. I won't play along. "Why do you suppose Angelo is so keen on managing our affairs?"

Julian sighs. "What would you have me say? That even decades after I stole you from him, he still wants to bed you?"

"If he makes the attempt, I'll feed him his manhood." Julian laughs, but I won't let him avoid this issue. "Do you ever worry that Angelo has too much power over you, that one day he will turn on you, and you'll be left with nothing?"

Julian's face grows somber and he looks away.

Now I feel sorry for drawing a cloud over the outing. Perhaps there is still time to repair the damage. "So tell me about this business venture we're undertaking."

Julian accepts my overture, his mood improving instantly. "We're meeting George Clymer, inventor of the

Columbian printing press."

"I haven't heard of it."

"It's a remarkable new hand press. Angelo may decide to invest in Clymer's expansion."

I do love the printed word. Perhaps this visit won't be as excruciating as I feared.

❧♥☙

The smell of paper and ink hangs heavy in Clymer's cramped shop. I love this scent. I became addicted while reading the biting political satires of Mercy Otis Warren during the first war. What a remarkable woman!

Clymer, an aging man with thick arms and a goatlike beard, stands proudly before his iron machine, extolling its merits. He shows us that with one pull of the handle, a single person can print an entire newspaper page!

The device is artfully designed. An iron eagle serves as a counterweight at the top of the frame. It clutches in its talons the thunderbolts of Jove, the olive branch of peace, and the cornucopia of plenty.

I marvel at our ability to disseminate the written word, revolutionary ideas, formed in the mind of one and shared by thousands. The printing press is our greatest achievement. It can topple kings and build new worlds. I reach out and touch the eagle. If this press remains in use for many years, churning out our thoughts day after day, perhaps this iron eagle will develop a soul of its own.

"Would you like to see her at work?"

I realize that Clymer is talking to me. I take my hand off the iron eagle. "I would."

I step back and Clymer eagerly sets up the machine. Julian is showing one of his impish smiles. I sense intrigue afoot!

After fussing nervously with the alignment of the paper, Clymer finally pulls the handle, drawing the press to the paper. He pulls out the sheet, waves it dry, and hands it to me triumphantly. "Have you ever seen anything printed so quickly?"

"I have not. Thank you, Mr. Clymer." I look at the paper and see that it's yesterday's *Democratic*, the local Philadelphia newspaper.

Julian looks over my shoulder. "What does it say?"

"Yesterday's news. The library expansion. A call to move the capital back."

"Anything else?"

His interest seems overly keen. This is the source of the intrigue! I look closer at the paper and notice a small article in the corner...

We are pleased to announce the fortieth anniversary of Cassandra Cross and Julian St. Fleur. The devoted couple became bloodmates in the year of our independence. Julian reports that his love for Cassandra has delivered him from a life of wretched loneliness. God willing, they will share another forty years, and another.

I feel a chill of panic. Has Julian lost his mind? He used our real names. Is our secret out? I turn away from Clymer and speak in the True Tongue. "What is this?"

"Have no worries, my love. It wasn't circulated. It's a special edition, just for you and me. Perhaps one day we can proclaim our love in public, but for now, this will have to do."

This was a reckless but romantic gesture. Typical Julian. I just pray that Clymer doesn't know the word *bloodmate,* or start asking how such a young couple could be celebrating their fortieth anniversary.

I throw myself into Julian's arms. "So you didn't forget our anniversary."

"Never. I simply waited a day to take you by surprise. I know how you abhor predictability."

My beloved Julian has a bit of the devil in him, just the right amount!

As we exit Clymer's shop, the smell of the waterfront cannot ruin my mood. I clutch the newspaper page to my heart, imagining where I will display it. Perhaps my bedchamber.

Our slumping carriage awaits, one wheel mired in the mud, and there's no sign of the coachman. Julian walks over to the horses to investigate.

Suddenly, the world spins around and around. I look up to see a man with a sword standing over me. Why is he upside down? My blood drips from his weapon, an intricately inlaid silver blade used by the Knights of Rome. A river of red flows across the ground, consuming my precious newspaper page and marking my exit from Mortalos.

The Knight has taken my head. He has taken my life with Julian. I look past this killer's sweating face and raven eyes, into his soul. I want to remember this man. I know I will see him again in a future life, and when I do, I will make him pay. May the hands of fate deliver him to me.

BERSERKIR

STEFAN HILDEBRAND

THE PRECEPTOR SITS behind her glass desk, waiting to know why I visited my family in Vermont. Fortunata, enjoying this immensely, laughs at me with her eyes. I knew there was a risk they'd track my phone signal, but going off the grid would pose even bigger questions. I don't want to look like I'm hiding from them.

I can't leave this office without providing a damn good explanation for my trip to Corby. What can I tell Stockhausen that she will believe? What do I actually know about her? Not much. Wait, her father is a KoR Commander out west somewhere. Did he pressure her to serve? Is she trying to make him proud? I sit back in my chair, taking my time before I speak. "I don't see my family much."

The Preceptor nods, her intense blue eyes never leaving me. "We're aware of that. We assumed you don't get along."

Now I go for the antacids. Have to make this look like I'm struggling with it. "My parents, mostly my dad, didn't want me to join KoR. He wanted me to take over our logging business."

Stockhausen leans forward, her face softening almost imperceptibly. A few locks of gray hair drop into her face, almost humanizing her. "So why visit him now?"

"I'm about to become a Knight. I wanted his blessing before I complete my quest."

Fortunata scoffs, but the Preceptor seems interested. "And did you get it?"

I stare at the floor, not answering.

Stockhausen thinks for a moment, then pushes back her chair. "Carry on, Hildebrand. You're both dismissed." She stands, straightening the blouse of her black uniform.

As easy as that? I must have pushed the right button. I nod my respect and head for the door. Fortunata, walking at my side, looks like she just drank a warm glass of chewing-tobacco spit.

After we pass the ant map and leave the office, Fortunata gestures me to an isolated spot in the hallway near a humming vent. I doubt she'd try anything stupid on Level Black, so I follow.

She leans in, whispering through a razor smile, "Why don't we settle this ourselves? Just you and me?" She smells like licorice and gunpowder.

So, the direct approach. "You want a duel?"

"To the death. Midnight, at Island Cemetery."

I nod. "No weapons, no armor."

Her dark eyes assess me. "No weapons, but I'm wearing silverweave."

Does she suspect I'm a werewolf? More likely she thinks I'll cheat and bring a weapon. I nod in agreement. "Get your affairs in order."

She grins, looking more relieved than frightened, then turns her back on me and stalks away. Her body recedes into the dark hallway, but I can still see the lights reflecting on her short black hair. She puts something shiny on it so it never moves. Not a single hair on her body is allowed to disobey her will.

Out in the Fort Adams motor pool, a bored KoR attendant hands me the key to a company car, a plain gray sedan. I convince him to give me another car. I don't want to drive what I was scheduled for, in case there are surprises inside.

After disabling the GPS tracking in the replacement vehicle, I throw away my KoR phone and activate a pre-paid phone purchased under an alias. I drive north out of Newport, pass up through Providence, then come south and re-enter Newport from the west, across the Pell Bridge. Convinced that I don't have a tail, I finally begin the task of finding Emma.

There's no way in hell I'm going to this *duel*. Fortunata has no intention of fighting me in the open. It will be an ambush. Let her waste her time setting that up while I look for Emma.

I spend the morning checking out every mansion and museum in Newport. There's no sign of Emma, so I widen my search.

In the Artillery Company Museum, they have a small exhibit of uniforms from different wars. I see a painted statue of an artilleryman from the Revolutionary War. Something about it bothers me. Is it the red cuffs? They seem too long. And how would I know that? Weird, I must have seen some documentary.

Out of ideas, I do a circuit of the Cliff Walk, a seaside path along Easton's Beach. Feeling energized by the smell of saltwater, I make another pass and pick up Emma's scent at the Forty Steps. It's faint, nothing trackable. She must have been here the day before.

I talk to the locals and run across a city worker named Carlson who clams up as soon as he sees my badge. I get the feeling he knows something but isn't telling. If I had more time, I'd find a way to pressure him. I can still do that later if I come up empty.

In the afternoon I take a second run at the mansions, hoping to find a different set of tour staff to question. At The Breakers I find an old lady who looks like she wants to slap my hand with a ruler. She complains about a girl who crashed her tour. This girl was asking about mansions that were off-circuit. It's Emma; I know it! My first good lead.

If you're on the run and don't want to be found, don't piss people off, especially someone like this old bitch, because they'll remember you and be the first to sell you out.

There are a lot of mansions off the circuit, but my instinct is to start with the oldest ones first. I manage to find a pair of very old mansions in private hands, their estates adjacent to each other. One of them is abandoned, so as the sun sets, I drive onto the grounds of the occupied house. It looks like an old Swiss castle made of white stone, floating in an ocean of short green grass. It's well-kept and beautiful, in its way, but I can't shake an odd feeling of foreboding.

I drive across the long stone driveway and park my car in a roundabout. As I exit the vehicle, I see movement in two places. Something in one of the third-floor windows, and something standing in the shadows of an archway sheltering a big front door.

In the window above, the dying sun catches the face of a withered old man holding a pair of binoculars.

Raising my hands in peace, I slowly approach. A huge man emerges from the shadows of the archway. A guard. Why does this mansion need a guard? And not just any guard. I can tell from his smell that he's *Berserkir*.

The Berserkir are our were cousins, only they channel bears instead of wolves. They tend to be loners, more out of control in a fight. Mostly they either work security or become criminals. And they're unstoppable. Even using Ars Duellica, I'm not sure I could take one in a fight.

He steps out into the dying light, holding what looks like a medieval war hammer in each hand. I see facial scars through the thin patches of his beard. His hard eyes, a foot higher than mine, look down on me with suspicion. He hasn't invoked. If he had, he would have attacked by now. He wouldn't be able to stop himself. Even without his bear, his sense of smell is better than mine. He knows what I am and he speaks to me in a growl. "What'dya want, wolf?"

I don't even bother showing my phony badge. It would only make him angry. I don't want to make him angry. "I'm looking for a girl named Emma Rue."

"She ain't here. Move along before you get a hammer up your ass."

"This is Clan Corby business."

He steps back a fraction. Our name has some clout. "Look, friend, there's only two people here, me and the owner."

He's probably telling the truth. I don't smell Emma here. I should go check out the abandoned mansion.

The huge front door creaks open and the old man steps out, all bald head and terrycloth robe. The binoculars in his withered hand have day/night capability. This dude takes his surveillance seriously. He speaks in a croak. "Come inside."

There's something ominous about the invitation, but it seems he has something to tell me, so I follow him in.

My nose curls at the old man smell as I enter the mansion. He leads me into a room with a marble floor and a twenty-foot ceiling. Four huge chandeliers throw glittering light on the vast space. He directs me to a set of chairs before a wide hearth. As I sink into the soft leather chair, I realize it's the most comfortable seat I have ever taken.

As he sits across from me, a stony butler brings him a drink. He offers me one as well but I wave it off. A short distance away, the bear eyeballs me, pissed that I'm inside the house.

The old man sighs, and for a moment he looks like he's falling asleep. It's that comfortable chair at work. But then his eyes snap wide with anger. "My name is Marion Broadwell. And that is my wife, Elizabeth." He points to a painting hanging over the hearth, a beautiful blonde girl in her twenties.

I sense a long story coming, one that I don't have time for. "I'm Stefan Hildebrand. I appreciate your hospitality, Mr. Broadwell. I just have a few quick questions about a girl who may have been here, Emma Rue."

"*He* has her."

"Who, sir?"

"The creature who lives on the ramshackle property adjacent to mine. He has used many names over the years. The bastard took my Elizabeth half a century ago, and now he has your Emma."

"Creature?"

"He's a vampire, Mr. Hildebrand. Does that shock you? Do you think me mad?"

Shit, that makes sense. Emma has a vampire soul. She'd be drawn to her own kind. "No sir, I don't think you're mad."

"Before Elizabeth was taken, we had a child together, Alisanne, and Alisanne has given me a granddaughter, Audrey. They live upstairs, and I'll be damned if that monster will take either of them."

"You spoke to the police about Elizabeth?"

Marion scoffs. "That's not how he works, Mr. Hildebrand. The women *want* to be with him. He always finds a way to trap them with their own desires. Emma is lost to you, I'm afraid."

I've located my target. So it's time to leave this comfortable chair. "I appreciate the heads-up, Mr. Broadwell."

I rise and shake his dry, bony hand. He looks at me with a mixture of pity and frustration. His voice croaks like a messenger of doom. "If you continue this pursuit, you will die tonight." He sounds utterly sincere, and his prophecy troubles me.

Velvet Cuff

Emma Rue

I wake up drenched in sweat, gasping and clutching at my hot neck. I can still feel Cassandra's head being chopped off. Tears fill my eyes as I think about her awful murder. There was something about Cassandra's killer that seemed eerily familiar. The soul of the man. I've seen it before. But where?

It suddenly comes to me. Professor Leeks! No wonder I kicked him in the balls. He murdered Cassandra in his previous incarnation. It's a miracle I didn't try to kill him. If I had kept Cassandra's promise of vengeance, I'd be in jail right now.

I sit up in Cassandra's bed and find a note from Julian beside me…

I have ventured out to feed.

Julian! I remember him throwing me on the dining table. I think I passed out, maybe from lack of food and water. I check my clothing. My undergarments seem to be intact. I'm amazed he didn't take what he wanted. Maybe there's still a trace of "good Julian" left inside him.

I look around the room. There is junk food and a water bottle on the vanity. And on the floor nearby, a chamber pot! What is it with vampires and chamber pots? I don't care if you're immortal, use the toilet.

I'll just grab the food and try to escape. My mouth waters as I focus on a bag of potato chips.

As I slide from the bed, I feel a weight on my ankle. It's a velvet-lined cuff, connected to a chain! Julian, you sonofabitch.

I examine the cuff. It's light but unyielding. The chain connects to the heavy bed frame. I'm not strong enough to break out of this. Maybe I can pick the lock.

The chain is just long enough to reach the vanity. I open Cassandra's jewelry box and start looking for something with a long pin. I find the lyre brooch and ease the pin into the cuff's old-fashioned lock, built small, like something you would lock a diary with. The pin breaks off in the lock, hopelessly jamming it. I'm such a brilliant escape artist!

The door suddenly bursts off the hinges and I nearly have a heart attack. I watch in shock as Micah flies into the room in a cloud of splinters. "Micah?"

He speaks as his deep blue eyes scan the room. "Are you okay?"

What the hell is he doing here? I haven't seen him since we spoke in the coffee shop back in Providence. That was only a few days ago, but it seems like forever. I want to know why he's here, how he found me, but there's no time for questions. When I look at his soul I see something familiar and comforting. That will do for now. I try to keep the fear from my voice. "We have to get out of here. Quickly."

Micah scratches the stubble on his chin as he sizes up the cuff around my ankle. As he runs a hand through his scruffy hair, I realize how unlike Julian he is. Where Julian is dressed to kill, Micah is dressed to go camping. Where Julian is a man you hope will take you, Micah is a man you hope to take. Both are beautiful, in their own way, but Micah manages it without trying.

Micah gently leads me to the foot of the bed. "Crouch down here."

I have no idea what he's planning, but he seems confident, so I comply.

He pulls a gun from under his jacket. It has something attached to the end of the barrel. A silencer? I know that Micah used to be a soldier and probably knows how to use the weapon safely, but I don't like guns. "What are you doing?"

Without answering, he pulls the chain around to the side of the bed. I can't see him through the bed's heavy frame. I hear a clicking sound as the gun fires with barely a whisper.

Micah returns and hands me the broken end of the chain, still warm from the gunshot. "I might be able to spring the lock on that ankle cuff."

I whisper urgently. "He'll kill you if he finds you here. We have to leave. Now."

"Who'll kill me?"

"I'll explain later. Let's go."

I grab the bottle of water and bag of potato chips. That's a good start, but once we escape this place, I'm going to find an all-you-can-eat buffet and put it out of business.

As we exit Refuge d'Amoureux and race toward Micah's car, I feel that I'm forgetting something. "Wait!"

I can't see Micah's eyes in the darkness, but I can feel his confusion. "What's wrong?"

Síndóm! Is the green dagger still under the window where it fell? And what about Cassandra's copy of the Declaration of Independence? "Start the car. I have to get something."

He shakes his head firmly. "You're not going any-where alone."

I've only known Micah for a short time, but I feel as if I've always known him, always had him near. He follows me as I run around the corner of the house. I drop the water and chips and dig through the brambles under the window.

Micah holds up a flashlight to help me. The briers leave long scratches on my arms as I desperately grope for the dagger. It's not here! Neither is the Declaration of Independence. Julian took them, the bastard! At least I still have the heartblaze ring on my finger.

Micah makes a noble attempt to sound patient. "What are you looking for?"

"It doesn't matter. Let's go." As I turn to leave, I see the dim outlines of the dual angels guarding the tomb. I feel something drawing me there. Is it Angelo? He doesn't speak to me with words. I get no sense that he's awake and aware, and I can't see his soul through stone walls. But I do sense an oddly comfortable feeling. Is that his love for me? Then I hear a flat voice that chills me to the bone.

"Cassandra, you disappoint me."

I look up and see Julian's gold eyes staring down from the window above. I know something terrible is about to happen. Maybe if I agree to stay with Julian, he won't hurt Micah.

I push Micah away from me. "Get out of here!" But Micah doesn't move. In the dim light his face looks almost sleepy. How is he not freaking out right now?

Julian leaps through the window and lands like a cat on the ground before us.

I imagine what Micah must be planning. But will a gun even work on a vampire? Julian will surely kill him. I whisper urgently to Micah, "Don't."

Julian sizes Micah up, then turns back to me. "Thoughtful of you to bring dinner, but I've already eaten."

Micah shines his flashlight on Julian and pushes a button. The flashlight makes a low beeping sound and explodes with a wicked bright light. Even from the side, the light stuns and partially blinds me. I can only see a faint outline of Julian clutching his eyes as he screams in pain. He looks like he's standing in the middle of a nuclear blast.

The ground suddenly moves beneath me. I see the broken chain swinging freely from my ankle cuff. Micah is sprinting to his car with me in his arms. He feels incredibly strong. How can he run so fast? Is he also a vampire? That can't be. Julian is cold to the touch, but Micah is so warm.

I try to relax as Micah drives us off the grounds and into Newport. I sneak a look behind, somehow expecting Julian to pop up from the backseat.

Micah speaks, his voice calm. "He's not following us."

"What did you do to him?"

"Garlic, crosses, holy water, none of that shit works on a vampire. But they *are* sensitive to light. The sun gun burned his eyes, but he'll recover in a few days."

I shake my head in disbelief. "What kind of soldier were you?"

"You don't want to know."

"Why do you still carry a gun?" He ignores the question so I change the subject. "How did you find me?"

"Checked your phone—you called about the mansions."

"You had no right to go into my apartment." *It's such a mess!*

He shrugs. I look into his soul, still so familiar. He seems…conflicted. He really likes me, but he's hiding something. And he's in pain. I want to ask him more questions, to get to the truth. I'm suddenly worried about him. "Are you all right?" He doesn't respond, but I can tell the question startled him. I should be quiet for a while now.

I look out at the dark road and try to get my bearings. "We need to get back to Providence. My friend is worried about me. Her little girl, Kaya, tried to run away. And I need to get this cuff off. And we need to stop somewhere to eat." *So much for being quiet.*

Micah doesn't respond.

Are we going the wrong way? "Did that last sign say we're headed for Fort Adams?"

He remains silent. What the hell is he up to? His fingers twitch against the steering wheel; their odd motions seem familiar, like something from the past, from Cassandra's world.

Soul Cage

STEFAN HILDEBRAND

I really like Emma, but I wish she'd stop talking. This is the worst night of my life and I'm in no mood to chat. I'm still wondering if it was smart to tangle with that vampire. It was a risk doing it without invoking, but I didn't want to reveal myself to Emma.

Is the vampire someone from her past life? I didn't kill him because I don't believe in butchering paranormals. I've had to do it to keep my cover at KoR, but I avoid it if I can. Will this act of mercy come back to bite me on the ass? Shadow walkers can pop in from Velox, so there's no sound or scent to warn you. They're the ultimate assassins. And I just pissed one off and left him alive to seek revenge.

The turn into Fort Adams is just ahead. My stomach burns but I'm out of antacids. I imagine Emma in a soul cage. They shove her into the plaga coffin and slam the lid shut. I hear her muffled screams as the deadly gas fills the cage, killing her body. Her soul is released but can't escape the cage. She'll spend forever in that coffin, deincarnated, removed from the eternal circle of life. It's the worst fate I can think of.

I would miss her.

Emma looks out at the dark road. "I think we're going the wrong way. You need to bang a U-ey."

Time to decide. If I take the exit into Fort Adams, I'll become a Knight of Rome and be the most important operative the were have ever had. And Emma will meet a fate worse than death. But if I don't take the exit, I'll be the pariah of my own people, a wolf without a clan.

There are no good choices here. How did it come to this? I think back to the kid I used to be, spending summers prowling the woods. I loved the forest and it loved me. It was alive and it embraced me. I thought the whole world was like that forest. I really want to be that stupid boy again, that boy who had never met Emma. What is it about her that makes me doubt my mission?

I ignore the turn into Fort Adams and "bang a U-ey." The decision is made. It's not just Emma, I don't want to see *anyone* put in a soul cage ever again. Working with KoR is corroding my soul, and that's not a sacrifice I'm willing to make for Clan Corby or anyone else.

Emma is hungry and exhausted, so we've stopped at a seedy motel in Portsmouth. She sits on the vibrating bed, shoving down "stuffies," a type of stuffed clam we got to-go at a place called Fieldstones. We also stopped to buy a bolt cutter, and Emma picked up a new shirt to replace her ripped one.

I try to slip the bolt cutter around her ankle cuff but she's moving around too much. "Hold still."

She nods, looking away as I line the bolt cutter up for another try. I notice that her feet are bare now. They're kind of pretty. Odd, I've never noticed a girl's feet before.

I snip the cuff from her ankle and she hugs me, wildly happy, a clamshell in her hand. "Thank you!"

I recognize that behavior. A feeding high. Not eating for a couple of days will do that. I feel a little sad when she ends the hug. I like the feeling of her body pressed against mine.

She finishes a bottle of water and tosses it into the trash. "Wanna get some beah?"

"You mean *beer?*"

"Yeah. You're from away?"

I think she's teasing me with this Rhode Island slang. Even though I work in Newport, I never hear it. None of the KoR personnel in Fort Adams are actually from Rhode Island. "I'm from Vermont. And you're not old enough to drink."

She laughs. "I'm much older than you think."

I've got to get to business while she's still in a good mood. "Emma, we have to talk about something."

She nods, dropping an empty clamshell into the trash, then reaching into the box for another one.

"You have bigger problems than that vampire back at the mansion."

"His name is Julian."

"Whatever. Have you heard of the Knights of Rome?"

She suddenly stops eating. I hit a nerve.

She doesn't answer so I continue. "They hunt paranormals. I work for them. *Used to* work for them. My name isn't Micah, it's Stefan Hildebrand. And I'm not really a student at your school. That's just a cover. They sent me to get you."

Her nostrils flare, pupils dilate. A fear response. Her voice falls to a whisper. "They sent you to kill me?"

"Worse. They plan to imprison your soul, to take you out of the cycle of life. It's called deincarnation."

"But you're *not* going to help them?"

"No."

"Why not?"

"Because KoR wants to destroy all the things that make this world special. Including you."

She smiles a little, thinking. "Do you believe in past lives?"

"Yes. My people were once Norse warriors."

"The Knights of Rome killed me in my past life, when I was a woman named Cassandra Cross. Someday I'll pay them back for that."

"Let me guess—you were a vampire, mixed up with the dude I just blinded?"

She nods. "But I'm mortal now, so I can't understand why KoR is still after me."

"They're worried that you're remembering your past life."

She bites her lower lip as she mulls it over. "And now they'll be after you too, because you disobeyed them."

"Oh yeah, they'll want to make an example of me."

"I'm sorry about that."

"Don't be. Worry about yourself. Listen, Emma, you can't go back to your apartment or see any of your friends again. Your life as Emma Rue is over."

As she considers my words, tears flood her eyes. "That's all I have. What will I do?"

Should I hold her hand or something? I try to sound comforting. "We'll figure it out."

"They already killed Cassandra. Why can't they just leave me alone?"

Tears roll down her cheeks. I put a hand on her arm. Her skin is so soft. Is this enough to comfort her? I suck at this. I'm not made for giving comfort. I went from being raised by wolves to nine years of brutal KoR training. Nowhere along the way I did I get advice on how to make girls stop crying.

Shit, what am I going to do with her? I can't take her back to Corby; they might turn her over to KoR to ensure my knighthood. There are other Ulfhednar clans out there but I doubt I'd be welcome. No one wants a man who's turned against his pack. I might actually have a better shot with the Berserkir. They don't like wolves, but they like people who ignore the rules and follow their own path. I'd be a novelty there, the rogue wolf. I *might* be safe, but what about Emma? Would they treat her as prey?

Emma has stopped crying. Her voice has some toughness in it now. "I'm willing to give up the life I've built, if you can call it that. But first, I have to say goodbye to Kaya and Melita."

"Sure, give them a call."

Emma shakes her head. "Kaya's only five, and she's freaked out that I disappeared. She isn't sleeping. She tried to run away. She made me promise I would come to see her. I have to keep that promise."

An emotional reaction, not a logical decision. That sort of mistake will get you put in a soul cage. There's no way you're going back to Providence. I try to sound sympathetic. "We'll work it out in the morning."

She gives me a long stare. I can't read her face. Can she tell that I won't let her go back? Can she tell I'm Were? Does she even know Were exist? Maybe I should have told her, but it feels too early. I'll wait until she's calmed down, until she trusts me a little more.

I get up to inspect the security of the room. Two entrances, front door and bathroom window. The bathroom door swings out, so I secure it with a chair tilted under the handle. I do the same for the front door. KoR has a couple of portable monitoring and counter-breach devices, but I don't have any on me, and chairs work surprisingly well.

Emma watches me, reading me. I wish she would stop. I see my fingers dancing and will them to be still. I turn to her, trying to sound casual. "I want to sleep beside you tonight, to keep you safe. I won't try anything."

She laughs. "I'm going to take a shower."

What is she laughing about? The truth is, I want to be next to her because I don't trust her to stay. I'll keep my shoes and clothes on, in case she tries to bolt. For some reason, I suddenly imagine Emma naked in the shower. Damn, Library Girl is getting to me. How the hell am I going to get any sleep if I'm lying in bed with her? Just the thought of it is making me hard.

I try to think of the forest.

Secret Language

CASSANDRA CROSS

1781

EMMA'S PAST LIFE

A THOUSAND CANDLES blaze in the chandeliers that form
a crystal canopy over the vast ballroom. Over the years,
the Bowery has grown from a dirt trail into New York's
most prosperous thoroughfare, and this ballroom is its
crown jewel.

Heads turn as we sweep inside. Julian wears a French
silk waistcoat patterned in cerise and cream. I have chosen
a cream silk ball gown woven with blaze-dyed stripes and
a trim to match Julian's waistcoat. He felt that a bit much—
my divorce is not finalized—but I want the world to know
he is mine.

The Officer's Ball is being hosted by General Sir Henry
Clinton, British commander-in-chief. The mood is tense.
Rumors have been circulating that the Siege of Yorktown has
taken a dangerous turn for England. That is no small relief,
as my father is among the forces encircling Cornwallis.

Julian and I have moved to New York to avoid the fighting to the south. But there is also another reason to stay out of patriot territory. My husband Tom is an officer in the Continental Army. I want to avoid any awkward encounters, each a reminder of my betrayal. Social events such as these are a soothing balm. When the dancing begins, my dark thoughts abandon me, if only for a while.

Our invitation was arranged by the Black Rose Society. There are seven of our kind in attendance tonight, easily identified by the blazestone dyes in their clothing, the colors visible only to Transcendent eyes.

I nod politely to Lorance Sparkes, Governor of the Society's New England Domain, and whisper a greeting in the True Tongue. With his square jaw and noble bearing, Lorance looks like a great European king. He approaches and takes me by the arm. I expect Julian to be jealous, but instead he seems proud.

Lorance speaks, his voice deep and rich. "Lovely to see our newest prodigy in attendance."

I nod demurely. "You flatter me, Governor."

Lorance is the greatest soulreader of our age and has taken a special interest in me since discovering my talent. He says I have an astonishing grasp of soulsight for one so newly made, and that one day I will surely become a Noble in the Society. He has promised to work with me, to develop my gift. I wonder, however, if his motives are truly altruistic. I worry that he may be smitten with me.

After wine and pleasantries, my beloved Julian leads me

out on the floor to join a square. There are four squares tonight, so this cotillion will be quite the spectacle. Julian and I have practiced the steps for hours, but suddenly I can't remember any of them.

As the orchestra begins to play, I watch Julian on the other side of the square, eager for this French dance to bring him back to me. The movements are lovely, but at the beginning he will pair with another woman. The thought of it makes me angry, but these are the social conventions we must endure.

I look over at the man I will dance with first, a British officer who looks oddly familiar. I look into his soul and it freezes my blood. What I see defies all reason and expectation. It is my husband, Tom, wearing a disguise!

The dance passes in a queasy blur. Hopping and stepping, twirling and circling, holding hands and grasping arms. All with multiple partners. Being in the arms of Tom, then Julian, then a handful of strangers is distracting beyond belief. Suddenly I realize that no one is dancing except for me. Somehow I missed the end of the music. My disastrous performance has humiliated me, though the dancers are kind enough to ignore it. *Why is Tom here dressed as a British officer? What is his mission?*

General Clinton, exuding his starched charm, pulls Julian aside to discuss business. Ostensibly, we are in New York as importers supplying the British Army. But Julian actually knows very little about this business; I hope it's enough to convince the General.

I watch Tom, standing only yards away. He's given no sign that he recognizes me, nor I him. For his guise he has adopted an odd, fidgety persona, complete with a high-pitched laugh and an abundance of hand gestures.

I've never seen this side of Tom. He's quite the accomplished spy. Odd though, his gestures don't always match his words, almost as if his hands are having their own conversation.

Tom hazards a glance at me as he leaves the ballroom and enters a bustling kitchen where the servants are hard at work. A moment later a scruffy boy hands me a note that reads...

Kitchen pantry.

Tom wants a secret meeting! I look over at Julian, who is busy nodding his head at everything the General says.

I really shouldn't meet with Tom. But I've destroyed his happiness and I feel I owe him.

∽∽♡∽∽

Tom pulls me deep into the pantry, his fussy officer's persona gone. He feels my cold hands and tries to rub life into them. "You're so cold! Are you ill?"

He mustn't know of my transcendence. I pull my hands back. "I'm fine, Tom. Please don't worry."

He looks in the direction of the ballroom through half-lidded eyes. "How is *he* treating you?"

"Julian is a gentleman. You know that. Why are you here? The war is in the south."

"I've been tasked with keeping an eye on General Clinton. But his staff officers are suspicious, always watching. So I'm making my reports to Continental observers at events like these, in full view of the public."

"I don't understand."

He moves his fingers in the odd patterns I saw earlier. "I've developed a secret language, allowing me to communicate with hand gestures. Tonight I reported that the siege of Yorktown is far worse for the British than what we had first heard."

That buoys my spirits. I want this terrible war to be over. But it's odd that Tom is sharing his trade secrets, something he's never done before. Perhaps he's pleased for me to see him in his element, as something more than the scorned husband. In truth, I am impressed. He is brave and intelligent, all the things my father promised when he arranged our marriage.

Tom glances worriedly toward the kitchen. "I must speak quickly."

I understand why. If caught in a pantry with me, it would be awkward to explain to the British, and the ensuing scandal would jeopardize his role here.

Tom seems unable to start, so I urge him on. "Yes, what did you want to say?"

He looks at the floor, a sadness in his eyes. "I wanted to apologize for our marriage."

Apologize? The fault is mine. But I'm afraid if I interrupt him, he won't continue.

"I chose the wrong path into this. After saving your father's life at Bunker Hill, he felt indebted to me, and I used that debt to secure his blessing. I wasn't sure I could win your heart on my own. In war, I am without fear, but in love I am a hopeless coward. I shouldn't have used your father to leverage the marriage. For that, I am profoundly sorry. I want you to know that I've spoken with a lawyer in Plymouth about expediting the divorce. You'll be free of me soon. And though I've no right to ask, please grant me this one final request. Will you extend your forgiveness?"

And I thought he wanted to delay the divorce!

I suddenly realize that something is wrong. I can't hear anything out in the ballroom. Why is it so quiet? Have we been discovered?

The door to the pantry flies open. It's Julian, his face filled with anger as he glares at Tom. "What are *you* doing here?" His words sound like a prelude to murder. I have to turn his attention away from Tom.

I lead Julian out of the pantry. "Why is it so quiet? What's happening out there?"

"Cornwallis has surrendered to Washington. The British are finished."

Joyous news! Now my father will be safe. I share a celebratory embrace with Julian.

As Julian locks a possessive arm around my waist, I look back at Tom, his plea for forgiveness still unanswered. Tom has spent the last seven years risking his life for the

Continentals, and finally, with victory in hand, he has lost something even more precious than his country. As I look into his soul, I see the hopelessness of a man who has accepted his fate at the gallows. I have a terrible feeling that the next time I see him, he will be dead.

BEAST WITHIN

EMMA RUE

THE PRESENT

I WAKE TO FIND myself on the motel bed next to Micah. *No, his name is Stefan. That will take some getting used to.*

Last night I washed my underwear in the sink and hung them over the heater to dry. I think I freaked Stefan out by going to bed in the nude. He tossed and turned most of the night but is now sleeping soundly. A shaft of morning light streams through a hole in the drapes and reveals his unshaven face, ruddy cheeks, and scruffy dark hair. A part of me wants to poke him awake so he will open those sad blue eyes.

I look into his soul, a bit easier to read while he's sleeping. He is not a bad person, but he's done bad things, and whatever those were, they've taken a toll on him.

His fingers twitch in his sleep and it reminds me of last night in the car, when I saw his fingers dancing on the steering wheel. I suddenly put it all together. *Stefan was once Tom, Cassandra's former husband!*

Stefan's twitching fingers are not a nervous habit, it's the secret language Tom created to communicate while spying. Stefan probably has no idea why he's doing it.

I remember Melita telling me about the book that said souls tend to orbit each other across many incarnations. How many lives have Stefan and I shared together? How many times have I been the cause of his unhappiness?

Stefan is on the run now, trying to protect me. He's risking his own life to keep me alive. I feel the sudden weight of that responsibility. Here is a man, a good man, a brave man, a man who would die for me.

I think of Tom, standing in the pantry, begging forgiveness from Cassandra and never receiving it. She should have been asking for *his* forgiveness. Did she make a terrible mistake by choosing Julian over Tom? If I could speak to her now, I would ask her to reconsider. Julian turned out to be no great prize. Was she tricked by his vampire pheromones?

Stefan shifts in his sleep and his hand falls on my arm. His touch is so warm. I trace a finger over his strong hand. His electric blue eyes flutter open, sparkling in the light. Any second he will say something, and it will be back to business, we'll be back on the run. But I want this moment to last. Before he can speak, I lean in and kiss his red lips, hot against my mouth. "I forgive you." *That was for Tom, standing in that pantry, waiting for forgiveness that never came.*

He looks confused. "What?"

I answer Stefan with another kiss, carefully watching his soul. This is a man who has spent every moment of his life in total control. But there's a part of him that longs to be reckless and free, and I've just awakened it. His passion ignites and soon we are kissing as I tear his clothes off. I expect to see the scarred body of a warrior, but his skin is smooth and perfect, wrapped tightly over muscles like corded steel.

As he explores me with his mouth, his soul appears to … blossom, becoming larger, more colorful. I see the presence of another! He has a secret self, some savage force, a beast within. He's getting rougher now. It scares me, and it thrills me. Old Emma might have been running for the door by now, but this new Emma wants to stay. I've never seen this intensity from a man. It's incredibly exciting and I want to see where it goes.

As Stefan showers, I dress myself with trembling hands. I feel giddy and exhausted. I'll have bruises tomorrow, and what looks like a rug burn on my knee. But I'll treasure each of these little wounds, souvenirs of a sexual adventure that few women have ever experienced. Stefan isn't just a man; he's a force of nature, like a tornado. Once raging, he cannot be controlled, cannot be stopped. You either go along for the ride or get torn apart.

Afterward, as the storm faded, he was gentle and attentive, in no hurry to leave the bed. He spoke little but didn't have to. His soul said everything I needed to know.

We're on the verge of falling in love. That sounds crazy after knowing each other for only a couple of weeks, but the truth is we've known each other for centuries. And no doubt in some future life, we'll be together once again. That thought is comforting.

But I can't let myself think about Stefan right now. Kaya needs me. I still can't believe she tried to run away. That's just not like her. Stefan won't agree to me seeing Kaya. He'll say it's too dangerous to go back to my old life and he's probably right. I could convince him to come with me but that could get him killed. I don't want to argue with him and I don't want to see him hurt, so there's only one solution. I have to hurry, before he gets out of the shower.

I find his jacket on the floor and take his car keys from the pocket. I could set out on foot, but I have a feeling he'd catch up with me. If I take his car, I have a chance to outrun him.

I find his phone and look around in the settings. When I see his number, I memorize it. When this is over, I'll call and apologize.

I have to be smart about how I do this. Julian could be looking for me, or the Knights of Rome could have sent another person to kill me, so I can't go back to my apartment. They could also be watching Melita, so going to her place would be dangerous. So instead, I'll have someone at the library slip her a note at work, setting up a meeting at a place we've never been before. I'll be like Tom and channel my inner spy.

I feel a pang of doubt as I pull away the chair blocking the motel room door. I only have my learner's permit and haven't been behind a wheel for two years. I'm not certain I can reach Kaya in one piece, but I have to try.

Closet Monster

Cynthia Greene

I watch through Kaya's eyes as she plays in the ball pit of a greasy fast-food restaurant. *Bacteria pit* is more like it. I wonder how many of these children have received pinkeye in addition to the overpriced, fattening food. On each end of the pit stands a pair of mechanical wizards. Every few minutes a ball rolls out of their mouths and drops into the pit. I doubt the restaurant washes them first.

Seble keeps watch on Kaya while Emma speaks to Kaya's mother nearby. Upon seeing Emma for the first time, color me unimpressed. I wouldn't mind having her long hair, but she needs to button that blouse higher. Honestly, this is a family place, not a brothel.

Emma claims she's met a man and wants to go away with him for a while. Liar. She's running from *me*. Kaya's mother is trying to talk her out of leaving.

Having spent time with Kaya, I've come to understand that she's a clumsy child. Her mother has made no effort to get her involved in sports or other activities. I'm no longer certain that Kaya has the physical strength to kill Emma. I'm also worried that when Emma dies and Rowan captures her soul, the witch won't have any leverage to make Emma reveal the dagger's location. So I've come up with a better idea. I'll use Kaya to force Emma into handing over the dagger, and only kill Emma *after* I have the weapon in hand. Rowan will be impressed with my initiative. I'm so very pleased with myself!

An old blind man enters and sits near the ball pit. Oddly, one of the mechanical wizards locks up with its mouth half-open. The old man stares at Kaya from under the brim of a black ball cap. Those sunglasses and white cane aren't fooling anyone, mister. I know you're here to watch the little girls. Pervert. Why isn't her mother noticing this?

Emma and Kaya's mother stand and hug goodbye. The mother, who is clearly not happy, touches Emma on the nose. What is that about? Emma's not a puppy.

Emma hugs a sullen Seble, then approaches Kaya in the ball pit. Now is the time to act. I find myself nervous, hoping that Kaya can properly deliver the lines as we practiced. It was like trying to teach algebra to a dog. She is five years old, but having been raised in an adverse environment, she has the mind of a three-year-old.

Emma wears a sad smile. "I have to go away for a while, my little gigglemeister."

Kaya responds forcefully. "Don't go! I have to tell you my secret."

"What secret? Tell me!"

Kaya grabs Emma's hand and pulls her into the sticky mass of colored balls. Perfect, perhaps Emma will die of pinkeye.

Kaya leads Emma to a corner of the pit and whispers into her ear. "He wants me to tell you something."

Dear Lord, child, get it straight. *He has a message for you.*

Emma looks confused. "*Who* wants you to tell me something?"

"The closet monster."

Emma flashes a worried smile. "Kaya, you know there's no such thing as closet monsters."

Kaya frowns. "Yes, there is. He talks to me in the dark."

Stick to the script!

Emma grows more serious. "What does he say?"

Tears swell in Kaya's eyes. *Come on, girl, you're almost there!*

"He wants the green knife. He won't go until he gets it."

Emma's face grows pale. "How do you know about the dagger?"

Kaya begins to cry. "The monster told me."

Emma's mouth opens and closes, like a fish out of water. *Good, it's hitting her hard.*

"Kaya, what does this monster look like?"

Kaya shakes her head. "You can't see him. But he talks every night and he won't go away!"

Emma, now crying, hugs Kaya. "Okay, Kaya, he can have the dagger. Just tell me how to give it to him."

The plan is working! That new body is as good as mine.

Suddenly, the old blind man, who has somehow shuffled up next to us, leans into the ball pit and whispers something to Emma. Emma's eyes roll in fear and she stumbles back, falling into the balls and disappearing up to her neck as if devoured by quicksand.

This disgusting old pervert is ruining all my work. I leap from Kaya's head into his, determined to teach him some manners. Though I have no body, I feel a sudden pain, like a spike being driven into my ear. I can't see through his eyes. I can't hear through his ears. His mind is a dark hole that leads straight to hell.

Shaken, I jump back into Kaya while I still can. I don't understand what happened. I have a cold feeling, nearly lost to my memory. I haven't felt it since I was incarcerated at WF1 in Cranston.

Fear.

So Many Guns

STEFAN HILDEBRAND

THE BANK TELLER looks surprised and uncomfortable. Her fingernails tap against the polished black counter. "The entire balance, sir?"

"Yes."

"Excuse me, sir, I need a manager to approve this transaction." She disappears into a maze of wood-paneled cubicles while I wait, a line building behind me. I don't like people being behind me. I watch them in the reflection of the glass shield separating me from the teller.

I've never tried to make a cash withdrawal on the entire balance of my KoR expense account. Has it been flagged? Has it already been canceled? Will armed guards rush out at any moment? If not, then I'll take that as a sign that KoR hasn't figured out I've turned, and I'll take an even bolder step.

A pretty teller at the next window catches my eye and smiles. She makes me think of someone I'm really trying to forget. Emma.

I really liked her. I've been with women before, but this is the first time I've let my guard down. Emma was amazing in bed. Her technique was a little awkward, probably hasn't had much experience, but the connection between us was…profound. She understood me. She accepted me. And then she betrayed me.

Why did I let her in? Why did I give her the power to hurt me? I barely know Emma, so why are my feelings so strong? Did we know each other in a previous life? Have I been her vampiric thrall? Does she see me as a useful tool, something she can put on the shelf when she doesn't need it? Shit, how could I be so stupid? I never thought of myself as one of those guys who thinks with his dick, but now I have evidence to the contrary. I'm ten years older and wiser than Emma, and she still managed to play me. I noticed that she had looked in my phone menu before she left. I think she was trying to find my number. Does she expect I'll come bail her out when she gets in trouble?

My teller returns with a stern manager carrying a shit-load of cash in a tray. He looks like a snooty French waiter serving a gourmet meal. They're actually going to give me the money! KoR still thinks I'm loyal. So now it's time for the second, and most dangerous, part of my exit strategy.

As I drive into the Fort Adams lot in a rented car, I half-expect to see a tactical team converge on my vehicle. But it's business as usual. Normally, I'd be worried about explaining the loss of my assigned KoR vehicle. But after today, there'll be no need to explain that Emma stole it.

Fort Adams, the New England regional headquarters for KoR, has some of the best weapons, communications gear, and surveillance equipment found anywhere in North America. If I'm going to be on the run from KoR, I need to be well-supplied, so why not take those supplies from the people who'll be hunting me?

After defying my family, I can't go home again. Even if I could, KoR would look for me there. And when word gets around that I'm a clan traitor, no other Ulfhednar community will want me. So my options are limited. If I can make it up to Maine, there are two Berserkir clans there, both in remote areas. Maybe one of them will take me in. And if not, I'll head over the border and try to get lost in the Canadian wilderness. I can be like one of those old-time mountain men with the long beards, living out my life in solitude until one day an avalanche frees my soul.

I walk from the lot and reach the security check at the north gate. A sleepy guard waves me through. I'm beginning to think this crazy plan might actually work.

As I enter the ludus I nod my respect to a fresco of Aristarchus of Ostia, the founder of our art. Our world headquarters hold the secret fourth-century scrolls on which he wrote *Ars Duellica.* I've never seen them, but I have copies of medieval manuscripts, all owned by KoR, that explain the meaning of those ancient scrolls. My dyslexia made it hard to understand them, but I studied my ass off and now people come to me when they have questions.

The techniques of Aristarchus are proven in battle. He used gladiators to test his theories. Men died to bring us these fighting secrets. I never forget their sacrifice.

No classes are in session, so I take a moment to say goodbye to the training hall that could have been mine. How many thousands of hours have I spent here? I know every mark on this wooden floor. Row after row of training weapons stand in frames along the walls. I take a moment to draw a steel longsword with a rebated edge. Each of these weapons is an old friend. I remember this particular sword. No one uses it because it's blade-heavy. Like me, it's the outcast of the bunch.

Master Cobo enters the room, stroking his white beard and eying me with his serious expression. When I first started here, I thought he hated me. He made me work harder than everyone else. Now I know that he loves me, in his own way. I'm the son he never had, and his heir to the Ars Duellica program. My betrayal will hit him hardest of all. I can't leave without finding a way to say goodbye to him.

As Cobo looks at the sword in my hand, his lips turn down in a frown that I know to be a smile. "Just like you, Hildebrand, always picking the sword that strikes the hardest."

I can't think of what to say to him, so I simply nod.

"Have you found the girl?"

I don't answer. He will recognize a lie.

He claps me on the shoulder. "Ah well, you'll get her soon, I'm sure of it."

As he passes through the ludus, I speak to his back. "Thanks for the encouragement. And everything else."

The Master stops, then slowly turns, his face unreadable. "Don't thank me, thank the art. It has given you gifts you have yet to understand. Use them wisely." He nods his respect to Aristarchus as he exits.

Somehow, Cobo knows I'm leaving.

My body is heavy with the weapons tucked into my waistband and boots. My jacket pockets bulge with gear as I push a heavy cart filled with every piece of field equipment I could requisition or steal.

The trick is to move slowly, to do everything in the open. I take my time pushing the cart across Level Blue. No one gives me a second glance. Ahead lies the side exit that will get me closest to the parking lot.

Suddenly, I hear a familiar voice behind me. "That's a lot of gear for taking down one college girl."

Fortunata. Of course. Fucking Fortunata. Somehow I hoped she'd still be at Island Cemetery, crouched behind a headstone, waiting to ambush me when I showed up for our duel. I turn, my voice icy. "If you got a problem with it, talk to the Preceptor."

Fortunata approaches the cart and casually flips through the contents. She's an asshole but she isn't stupid. She's putting it all together. Even if I somehow manage to get past her, she will be the one leading the hunt for me, and she won't quit until she's dead.

I'll need to improvise here. At the exit ahead I see only one guard, and he's checking his phone. This is probably the best chance I'm going to get.

As Fortunata pulls one of the stolen items from the cart, I draw my suppressed .22 pistol with a subsonic load and squeeze a round into her forehead.

The click of the firing pin doesn't draw the guard's attention, but there are cameras everywhere, so I know this moment has been captured for posterity. The thing is, there are a lot of cameras, too many to have eyes on them at all times. With any luck, no one was watching at this very moment. And even when they view the footage later, they won't be able to tell I'm a shifter because I didn't invoke.

For the longest time, Fortunata stares at me with a look of utter surprise, and then she pitches noisily into my cart. The guard ends his call and approaches to investigate the clatter. He's wielding a close-quarters assault rifle and wearing full silverweave combat armor with a silverglass visor. Over his heart I see the KoR emblem, a golden laurel wreath on a red background. Every inch of him is bulletproof. I have so many guns, but none of them can touch him.

Brass Claws

EMMA RUE

I STAND IN the ball pit, feeling helpless as Kaya cries. "Kaya, you know there's no such thing as closet monsters."

She frowns. "Yes, there is. He talks to me in the dark."

It occurs to me that she's been talking quietly so that her mother, sitting over at the table, can't hear. I look into Kaya's soul. I see terror, and truth. And I see something else, something that is not Kaya. Whatever this creature is, it has found a way inside her. I feel a creeping ache in my gut. "What does he say?"

"He wants the green knife. He won't go until he gets it."

Blood rushes in my ears as my heart starts to pound. She's talking about Síndóm! As I speak, my voice comes out broken. "How do you know about the dagger?"

Kaya begins to cry. "The monster told me."

What is this monster? Julian? But that doesn't make any sense. "Kaya, what does the monster look like?"

She shakes her head. "You can't see him. But he talks every night and he won't go away!"

I don't know what Síndóm does exactly, but it's probably not a good idea to give it to this *thing*. But I don't care. I just want Kaya to be happy and safe. Julian probably has the dagger; I'll find some way to get it from him. I hug Kaya through the blur of my own tears. "Okay, Kaya, he can have the dagger. Just tell me how to give it to him."

Suddenly, an old blind man with dark glasses leans over into the ball pit and whispers in my ear. "Hello, Cassandra."

I gasp and look into his soul. I don't recognize it. But he smells like Julian! He must have used metamorphosis to disguise himself.

I stumble away from him and fall back into the ocean of balls.

Melita, upset by Kaya's tears, comes over to pull her out of the ball pit and hug her. "Emma isn't leaving forever. You'll see her again, I promise."

But I know Julian won't let her fulfill that promise. I feel his iron grip on my hand as he pulls me out of the pit and toward the exit. He's going to kidnap me in broad daylight! We're getting a few glances from the people in the restaurant but no one is alarmed. Julian makes it look like I'm guiding an old blind man to the door.

Melita is busy with Kaya and has her back to me. I think of calling out, but knowing Melita, she will start hitting Julian and things will get out of hand. Better to cooperate with him. I need him to give me Síndóm.

As I drive away from the restaurant, I accidentally cut off a woman with children in the car. She honks and flips me off.

Julian sits in the passenger seat beside me, his steely fingers around the back of my neck. "You're a terrible driver."

My hands are shaking and I take a deep breath to still my racing heart. "How did you find me?"

"I followed your friend. She wasn't hard to locate. You telephoned her from my home." Julian takes off his dark glasses and rubs his bloodshot eyes. "With my eyes still recovering, I opted for this disguise. Perfect, is it not? Everyone stares at a blind man, but no one sees him."

It's time to get some answers. "Did you tell Kaya about Síndóm?"

Julian glares at me. "I don't speak with mortal children."

"Then who's been talking to her?"

Julian stiffens and I realize I've just run a red light.

He speaks to me like I'm a child. "Take care. I can survive an accident, but I doubt that you can."

"Just tell me what's going on with Kaya!"

He removes his hand from my neck. "As a mortal, your soulsight is weakened, or you would have noticed that she wasn't *alone.*"

Condescending bastard. "I did notice. What was that?"

"There is a spirit within her, a powerful one, I'd say, based on its attempt on me. Likely a minion of Rowan's."

"Who's Rowan?"

"An age-old Irish hag. Empress of Witches. Apparently the dagger belonged to her before it was stolen and released on the gray market, where I found it."

"What does it do? Why is it so important?"

"I've no idea, and I couldn't care less."

"If Rowan's the one who's tormenting Kaya, you have to give the dagger back to her."

A predatory grin crawls onto his phony old man face. I see that he has managed to make his teeth look yellow. "I will consider assisting you in this matter, but only if you prove more … cooperative."

I will do anything to protect Kaya. "What do you want?"

"Begin by taking us home."

Julian, still in his old man form, leads me into Refuge d'Amoureux. The familiar smell of rot and mold assaults my nose. I never thought I would willingly return here. At least it's a little brighter now. He's restored the power and turned on a few dusty lamps.

Julian leads me up the creaking stairs to the third floor, a level that didn't exist in Cassandra's time. The faded wallpaper is filled with little pink bunnies. I think I've seen that pattern on a diaper.

He speaks in a surprisingly sad tone. "This floor was an addition. I built it for Elizabeth."

"Who's Elizabeth?"

"You'll meet her soon enough."

I don't like the sound of that.

Julian leads me into a large bathroom lit by a lamp painted with pink carnations. The room looks like something from an elegant bygone era: a pink-and-white checkered floor, and glass faucet handles for the sink, one for hot and one for cold. A huge bathtub dominates the corner, perched on brass claws. A layer of dust covers everything like a blanket of snow.

Julian pushes me toward the tub. "The water has been restored. You will bathe now. I can't tolerate the smell of that wolf on you."

"Wolf?"

"Yes, your Were savior."

"You mean, like a … werewolf?"

"Yes, I mean a werewolf. Are you listening?"

Stefan's a werewolf! That would explain his behavior in bed and the strangeness of his soul. Why didn't he tell me?

What's happening to my life? A week ago I was living in a normal world, surrounded by my books. Now I've fallen down some rabbit hole filled with dangerous supernatural creatures.

Julian's snapping voice pulls me away from my thoughts. "Well? Get started!"

"I'm not going to bathe while you're watching."

He makes a hissing noise. "So you'll spread your legs for a wolf but won't even bare your skin for the eyes of your eternal love?"

If I had a bat right now I'd smash his old man face. How dare he mock what he and Cassandra once had? That was a genuine romance, not this slavery he wants now. I'm so angry at him. Words fail me.

Julian glares. "Wash the stink of him from your body or taste my wrath."

He marches out. I close the mirrored door, use a wet towel to wipe the dust from the tub, and start the water running.

I have to use this time to think. Julian has too much power over me. There has to be a way to even the balance.

I find some sort of lavender oil for the bathwater. It turns the bathroom into a fragrant garden. I remove my clothes and sink into the warm water. It feels heavenly. The tub is so large that my feet don't touch the end. Floating in this warm cocoon, my mind drifts to Cassandra.

Thorn Cradle

CASSANDRA CROSS

1794

EMMA'S PAST LIFE

I LIE ON A STRAW BED in a rustic cottage as a sweating artist works by candlelight to ink a black rose tattoo over my heart. Julian, upset with me, paces about. I'm wearing a thin red linen gown without a chemise. He insisted that I wear something more substantial to protect me from the ordeal to come, but I felt it important to demonstrate my courage to the Black Rose Society.

Lorance watches from the foot of the bed, his sharp eyes following the artist's work. Lorance also bears a black rose tattoo over his heart, the symbol of a Society Noble. I am the youngest Noble ever to be initiated, largely because Lorance has taken a personal interest in me. My greater power is soulreading, which evolved from the normal Transcendent power of soulsight. Lorance is a soulreader as well, and Julian believes that Lorance is grooming me to one day take his place at the head of the New England Domain.

Most members, including Julian, never receive titles. To earn a single rose and the title of Master or Mistress, a Transcendent must develop and demonstrate a greater power. To wear two roses and be declared a Lord or Lady, two greater powers must be mastered. One such person is Lord Trumbull, ruler of the North American Realm. Three roses declare a King or Queen, and there is but one at present, Queen Dauphinais in France. I hope to meet her one day.

The artist finishes the tattoo and looks to Lorance. As governor of this domain, his approval is far more important than mine. Lorance rubs his square jaw. "Acceptable."

High praise from Lorance. The artist smiles. "Thank you, sir."

To the mortal eye, the tattoo appears to be a simple black rose. But the Transcendent eye can see the blaze-stone ground into the inks, making the rose petals pulse with blood-red veins. These are the luscious colors of the dark spectrum.

The tattoo hurts, but it is nothing compared to the pain to come. Julian tells me he once witnessed a Transcendent suffer horribly in the thorn cradle. It took her months to recover. The truth is that I am frightened of this ordeal, but even more frightened by the prospect of disappointing Lorance and bringing shame to Julian.

Lorance gently re-laces my gown, covering the new tattoo. "We're very pleased you have decided to embrace this rite of passage. As a Society Noble, you will henceforth be known as Mistress St. Fleur. Now that you are a soulreader, you must understand that your own soul has been changed forever. The power of soulreading will remain with you for every incarnation to come. So forevermore, regardless of your parentage, you will be Mistress St. Fleur."

"By your leave, Governor, may I be known instead as Mistress Cross?"

Lorance looks to Julian, who nods his assent. This has never been an issue for Julian. He understands my wish to honor my father.

Lorance continues in a regal tone. "Very well, Mistress Cross. I will leave off with this. There are new threats at our door. A group known as the Knights of Rome has migrated from Europe, set on thinning our ranks. They will no doubt take an interest in you. And though you must concentrate on such problems within the Society, always remember that your first responsibility is to your Maker. Regardless of your station, he will always remain your lord and master."

I take Julian's hand and smile, recognizing the truth of the governor's words. Julian is my life, my world. There can be no happiness without him. But Julian doesn't share my smile. He looks distressed. He is worried for my safety in the ritual to come, and it makes me love him even more.

Outside the cottage, a steep hill rises in the ruddy light of a blood moon. Crickets chirp as Lorance leads us to a nest of long-thorned black roses tangled at the base of a rocky cliff.

The cradle of thorns.

Julian grimaces as I reach into the serpentine tangle of beautiful and deadly flowers. Blood beads on my hand in half a dozen places as the thorns quench their thirst.

Julian speaks to me in the True Tongue. "This isn't necessary, Cassandra. The Society recognizes your power. You've nothing to prove to anyone. I beg you to reconsider. Even an immortal can perish here, and I've no wish to live in a world without you."

I apologize with a kiss. There is no point in arguing with him. He already understands my reasons. A leap into the cradle is an ancient rite of passage, endured by all titled Transcendent.

Lorance gives me a questioning look, one last chance to reconsider. Does he really expect me to falter now? "I'm ready, Governor."

Lorance nods his approval and makes a hand signal. A dozen Society members, wrapped in black canvas and carrying heavy shears, emerge from the shadows and surround the thorn cradle. They will be the ones to free me when it is done.

I hug Julian for what I pray will not be the last time. "I love you."

He doesn't respond, not trusting his voice. I see tears in his eyes. Julian is very brave and would no doubt laugh off his own impending doom, but when it comes to my safety, he is not so cavalier. He waits behind as Lorance takes my hand and leads me on a broken, vine-choked path that leads halfway up the hill.

The path emerges on a ledge a good ten yards above the cradle. Heights have always frightened me, and I become lightheaded as I venture a glance below. Quickly, I turn my eyes to the starry sky above and the vertigo passes.

As Lorance steps away, I have never been more afraid. I think back to when my father joined the Continentals. My family cried as he departed, certain they would never see him again. I cried as well, but I also gave him a warm travel coat, made by my own hands. If he had to leave, I wanted some part in it. It was my way of taking control of fate, and it gave me comfort.

Once again I feel the need to control fate. I know that Society members are envious of Lorance's interest in me. Most feel I am too young to receive this honor. So I must leave no doubts as to my commitment.

Lorance looks alarmed as I back away from the ledge and return to the hillside. Below, Julian smiles in relief. He thinks I have reconsidered.

But instead of returning to them, I leave the path and continue higher up the hill.

Julian calls from below. "For God's sake, Cassandra, what madness is this?"

I don't dare respond, knowing my voice will waver.

I reach the crest of the hill and step to the top of the cliff. From twenty yards above, the thorn cradle looks very small indeed. What if I miss the mark?

Julian's voice sounds broken. "That's too high! Please,

Cassie, I beg you."

He could step into Velox and be at my side in a blink. But he stands his ground. It's the bravest thing he's ever done. I'm so in love with him. I don't want to die. But I do need to perform an act that will vanquish my doubters and leave the Society talking for centuries.

I think of Julian as I spread my arms and fall forward. I feel the hands of fate reaching out for me.

Rat Brothers

STEFAN HILDEBRAND

THE GUARD at the Fort Adams exit wears bulletproof silverweave armor and carries a standard-issue KoR close assault rifle coated in blacksilver paint, loaded with silver-core 5.56mm bullets. He stinks of silver.

I look into his visor. He has a lean face with bulging eyes. I know him. Varga, Vega, something like that, an older guy who never squired. He took a class from me a while back. Wish I could remember his weaknesses. With any luck, I can get out of this without a fight.

With the cart full of gear between me and him, he can't see the gun in my hand. I let the .22 drop onto my foot to hide the sound of it falling as I push the cart forward with Fortunata's body slumped inside. There's surprisingly little bleeding from her head.

I try to think of a believable lie. For a minor wound, we'd take her to the infirmary, but not for a gunshot to the head. "Open the door. I have to get her to a hospital."

He recognizes me and relaxes a little. "What happened?"

I use my best command voice. "Intruder. They've got him pinned down on the other side of the elevator. Open the door."

He nods and opens the door. As I push the cart out, he sees the treasure trove of gear under Fortunata's body and raises an eyebrow. "What's all this stuff?"

Now he's suspicious. There's no way he'll stand by as I load all this crap into my trunk. I have to do this right. He has to be dealt with, but he doesn't deserve to die for being at the wrong door at the wrong time.

As I approach him, the urge to invoke is almost overpowering, but that's something I *really* don't want on the security cameras. I lower my voice, stepping closer to him. "Let me explain…"

Now I'm inside his reaction time. I sweep his rifle barrel to the left and power my free hand up between his arms, grabbing the stock and violently shoving the weapon out of his hands.

Without missing a beat, he steps across me with his left foot and wraps his arm around my waist for a hip throw, but he's not close enough to get a good set. I kick his left leg out before he can execute the technique. He goes down and I smash the rifle butt into his knee. The pad in his armor drives into his knee, breaking his kneecap. He'll be okay in a couple of months. Without that armor though, he would have had a lifelong limp. As he groans in pain, I speak softly to him. "Stay down. I don't want to kill you."

I retrieve my .22 from the floor and throw it in the cart along with the rifle. Then I toss Fortunata's body to the floor and race for the parking lot, shoving the bouncing cart toward my vehicle.

The fallen guard is out of sight now. He's probably already called for help. I doubt it will arrive in time to stop me. I'm liking my chances of getting out of here alive.

As I head west out of Newport on the Pell Bridge, I mentally complete an after action report, assessing my performance. The truth is, it went well. I made my peace with Master Cobo, took out my most dangerous enemy, and escaped with a half-million dollars' worth of KoR gear, enough to wage my own private war. It had all been easier than I thought. Maybe too easy. Did KoR *allow* me to escape for some reason, or did I just get lucky?

I'm worried about Fortunata. She has plagued me for so long; could she really be taken out so easily? After the guard was neutralized, I should have emptied the entire clip into Fortunata's head, just to make sure she was dead. Evil like that needs a few extra bullets.

An hour later I pull over outside of Putnam for gas. Now that I'm in Connecticut, I'll work my way up to Maine. Visiting my family in Vermont is out of the question. KoR will have people watching. I can't afford to do anything predictable.

As I wait for the tank to fill, I look across the street at a run-down appliance repair shop. A pair of boys, brothers from the look of their matching rat faces, are abusing an unhappy cat. They whoop as they shove the animal into a rusty oven sitting alongside the old shop. One of the boys giggles as he turns up the heat. *Stupid kid, it's not even plugged in.*

I can hear the cat's muffled howl as the boys leave. How long, I wonder, before they let it out? What if they forget about it? A sick feeling pinches my gut. I think of the soul cages back at KoR. Would they be shoving Emma into one of them soon?

A worried older girl approaches the oven and frees the cat.

Who would be there to free Emma?

I look at my mobile phone. What if Emma has been trying to call? I threw away my old phone and she doesn't have this number.

Maybe I should call her, just to see if she's okay. How stupid would that be?

FRAGFACE

CYNTHIA GREENE

ONCE AGAIN, I see through Rowan's eyes as she sits in the dark room before her candlelit mirror with the gilded frame. She wears the mask of twisted leaves and stares into the mirror with eyes like frosted emeralds. I've made my report and Rowan is not pleased. She speaks with a voice threatening violence. "Where is Emma Rue now?"

"I'm not sure at the moment, but—"

Rowan interrupts. "You disappoint me, Cynthia Greene. I gave you a simple task and you've introduced unnecessary complications."

"I'm sorry, Mistress. I thought if…"

Rowan jumps in, voice cracking like thunder. "You *thought*? You do not think, you obey! You were told to kill Emma Rue and find out what you could about Síndóm. You were *not* told to retrieve the weapon yourself."

I've never seen her so angry. Has she changed her mind about giving me a body? "Yes, Mistress, I'm very sorry."

Rowan half-closes her eyes; blue glitter flashes on her eyelids. "My first instinct is to set you adrift in the metaverge. But as I pause and reflect, I think that too soft a punishment. So instead, I'll send you back to that prison."

Oh Lord, no! Not that horrible prison! It's operated by animals. Each day brings some new torment. "I deeply apologize, Mistress. I beg you for one more chance. Please, Mistress, I can still succeed!"

She stares at her own image in the mirror, as if staring into my soul and finding it lacking. A thin spiral of dark smoke rises from her candle.

Rowan finally speaks after an eternity of silence. "Very well, I'll give you one final chance to finish her. And this time you'll have a body to use."

A body! How exciting! I hope Rowan will let me keep it. I would like to be a blonde this time, with pretty blue eyes!

Her voice cracks like broken bone. "Fail me again and you'll pay a terrible price. That's for certain."

I awaken inside a dark, stinking enclosure. I know I am in a body, but oddly, I can barely feel it. Everything is numb. I try to rise to my feet and my head hits something metallic. That should have hurt, but it doesn't. The metal gives way, a lid of some sort. I push it up and discover that I'm in a dumpster filled with brown lettuce, moldy bread heels, and half-eaten pasta crawling with flies.

I look at my body. The body of a man! What evil has Rowan done? I wanted the body of a great beauty, but instead, I have hairy knuckles stained with dried blood. I struggle out of the disgusting dumpster into some back alley filled with litter and debris. What an eyesore.

I find it difficult to maintain my balance. This body wears torn jeans and tightly laced combat boots. His stinking sweatshirt is stiff with dried blood. I tear it off and discover a muscled torso beneath. He has three stab wounds in his chest, one of them over his heart. How could he survive that?

With a sinking sensation, I put my numb hand over my neck to feel for a pulse. Nothing. Still and cold. I press my finger into the gaping heart wound. No pain, no bleeding. This man is dead, apparently murdered!

I check his pockets for identification and find them empty. On his right forearm he has a blood-colored tattoo that reads *Fragface*. Is that his nickname? Oh dear. On the side of his left bicep is a black tattoo. This one reads *U.S. Ranger* and shows a skull in front of crossed rifles. So this was a man who lived by the sword and died by it. Perhaps his murder was justified; perhaps he was a brute and a bully who finally got what was coming to him.

On the ground next to the dumpster, I spot a car's broken-off side mirror. I pick up the mirror. I'm afraid to look at this man's face, but it has to be done.

I gaze into the mirror and see the fractured image of an abomination.

His hooded eyes are surrounded by a face that looks as if it's been cut apart and sewn back together in a random order. Fragface, indeed. If this is the best that medical science can achieve, then humanity is doomed. On the other hand, he's made of flesh, and he's mine. It's better than being a ghost.

Farther down the alley, a fat man in a dirty white apron emerges from a back door and empties trash into another dumpster. He uses his foot to keep the door from closing behind him. As he catches sight of Fragface, he goes pale and his foot slips from the door, allowing it to shut. He speaks with a nervous quaver. "You all right, pal?"

Can I make this body speak? My voice comes out in a croak. "Help me." I set Fragface stumbling toward the fat man, who tries to run back inside, only to find that he's locked himself out. His trembling hands fumble for the key chain hanging from his belt.

I need the fat man. I need his shirt and any money he might have. Perhaps I can beat him into submission. But unlike my new host, I don't know anything about fighting. Fragface's body feels eager to attack, so I simply relax and let his muscle memory take over. His meaty fist catches the fat man on the side of his jaw, snapping his head around with a popping sound and knocking him cold. His dirty apron catches on the door handle and tears as he drops to the ground.

What a remarkable display of violence! I've never felt that kind of power before. So this is what it's like to be a man, crushing your enemies and taking whatever you like. I could become accustomed to this.

I take the fat fellow's shirt and wallet. He has a bit of cash, a credit card, and a Rhode Island I.D. with a Providence address. Excellent, I'm already in the city so I won't need to travel far to find Kaya and her mother. Fragface can make them tell me where Emma has gone.

LOVE GAMBIT

EMMA RUE

I GRASP AT the black thorns puncturing my body. It takes me a moment to realize that I've awakened from my dream and I'm floating unharmed in Cassandra's big bathtub. I take a deep breath of lavender-scented air, trying to slow my racing heart.

I touch the heartblaze ring on my finger. Cassandra was so reckless and brave. It was her love for Julian that gave her the strength to jump into that bed of thorns. I've never felt that way about anyone. It must be incredibly empowering.

I think back to what Lorance said. Julian, as Cassandra's Maker, would always be her master. Does this mean he'll try to control me in every future incarnation? What about Julian's master, Angelo, the vampire he trapped in the tomb out back? Angelo was Julian's Maker, but Julian somehow defeated him. If Julian found a way to best his master, then I can find a way to best Julian.

I flinch as Julian, now returned to his true form, suddenly sweeps into the bathroom. "You've passed the day away in here. I thought perhaps you drowned."

"I've been dreaming about Cassandra. Do you remember the cradle of thorns?"

"No." His voice sounds icy and distant. He takes a thick pink towel from the rack and shakes the dust from it.

How could he have forgotten? More likely he's just trying to be difficult. I look into his soul, finding nothing but a distant stir of unreadable emotions. "She couldn't have made that jump without you. You meant everything to her. And I know you felt that way about her. Wouldn't you like to feel that way again?"

"No."

What an extensive vocabulary he has. He holds up the towel for me to step into. I see his eyes feasting on my body as I prepare to emerge from the water. "Don't look at me."

"I'll look where I please."

This is hopeless. If I stay in the tub, he'll only drag me out. I cover myself with my arms as I step out and into the towel.

Suddenly I feel Julian's third hand creeping up my leg. Oh what a gentleman he is. As I pull away, my voice comes out louder than I intended. "Stop it!"

He slaps me. "You will speak to me with respect."

My cheek throbs with warmth where he hit me. How can this be the same man who gave Cassandra the strength to leap into the cradle of thorns? If she could see him now, she would be disgusted, and she certainly wouldn't tolerate his crap. I try to put some steel in my voice. "I will speak to you with respect when you start treating *me* with respect."

He shrugs. I feel his third hand leave me. "The rags you are wearing simply won't do. Let's get you a proper dress."

Holding the towel around myself, I slip my wet feet into my flats and Julian leads me back down to the second level.

Julian opens a room that I don't recognize from Cassandra's memories, a gigantic closet filled with dozens of colonial-era dresses, all of them in perfect condition. I see a pale green gown, a pink, silk chiffon dress with an embroidered floral bodice, and a blue silk gown with layers of ruffles.

Julian opens a chest of drawers. "Your undergarments are here. Over the years, I've had everything repaired or replicated. All are exactly as you left them."

Getting him to see me as Emma is a lost cause. Maybe that's good. It might actually help with my new plan. Now is the time to be bold. If he wants to see some skin, I have plenty of it. I slide off the towel and reveal myself to him. "Assist me, please."

Julian nods approvingly as he drinks in the sight of my body. "Certainly, my gem."

He helps me sort through the strange assortment of underclothes. It must have taken women forever to dress in those days. As he laces up a corset, or what Cassandra called a *stay,* I speak with a casual tone. "Julian, do you remember that night on the roof?"

He shakes his head.

"The night we became bloodmates. Do you remember

what we did in bed? Do you remember conventus?"

"That was long ago. Why would I remember?"

Such a sweet, charming man. "It was amazing. Something only two vampires can share."

He frowns. "You will not use that vulgar word. I am Transcendent."

"I'm sorry." I point to the pale green gown. "That one, please." He helps me into the gown. It smells like cinnamon. "My point is that a mortal partner like me can't compare to a Transcendent."

He shakes his head. "I know what you're thinking, but I can't elevate you. You've already been one of us. If you try again, you will die. Each soul has but one opportunity for Transcendence, and you've had yours."

My heart sinks. As a mortal, I will be forever at his mercy. Exactly what he wants.

Julian steps back and looks at the gown. "Acceptable, I suppose. Now find some proper footwear."

I turn to a selection of colonial shoes along the far wall. I see a faded pair of salmon-colored shoes with low heels and a rusted buckle, a pair of white leather shoes with a similar heel but no buckle, and a pair of backless wine-colored mules with a moderate heel.

I pick up the white shoes and find the leather stiff in my hands. I don't even have to try them on. They're too small. My feet are enormous compared to Cassandra's. I feel like an elephant. My voice comes out weaker than I intended.

"They're too small."

Julian rolls his eyes. "Never mind, then, wear your own. Come, I've prepared a meal for you, and later, an exhilarating evening."

What does he mean by "exhilarating"?

Julian leads me down the grand stairs and into the Great Hall of Refuge d'Amoureux. My giant ape feet nearly trip over the long skirt of my gown. How did women ever get around in these things?

A shaft of sun from one of the tall windows lights a dusty space at the long table, revealing a single place setting. That must be for me. I see a crystal goblet filled with a red liquid. It had better not be blood! My plate is covered with a tarnished silver lid that hides its contents. I'm not sure I want to know what's under there. I'm hungry though. I was too upset at the restaurant to eat with Melita and the kids.

I feel bad about the way I left it with Kaya. Should I have told Melita the truth about what's been happening to me and Kaya? Would she have had me committed? If a friend told me that story, I would think she'd lost her mind.

Stefan is the only person who can know the truth, and I've treated him badly. It suddenly occurs to me that he may come back here looking for me! Julian will be ready for him next time. I can't let that happen. I need to apologize to

Stefan and keep him away from this place.

As we approach the long table, I release Julian's hand and try to speak with casual confidence. "Before I eat, I need to call Stefan."

Julian frowns. "Your wolf?"

Wolf. That will take some getting used to. "I need to tell him I'm here of my own free will, and that I'll return his car when I can. If I don't, he may show up here and kick the door in."

Julian flashes a wicked smile. I expect to see fangs, but there aren't any. "I'll be certain to show him the hospitality he deserves."

I push the fear from my voice. "No. I won't have you hurting my friends." Was Stefan my friend? Something more? Or perhaps he's an enemy now.

Steeling myself, I turn away from Julian and walk out of the Great Hall. At any moment I expect to feel him grabbing me from behind. But he doesn't. I realize that when I'm more assertive, he seems to treat me better. But there is a line, and if I cross it, he will hurt me.

I reach the foyer and pick up the phone. I call the number I memorized in the motel room. Suddenly I'm nervous. What will I say to Stefan? How will I explain what I've done?

His phone rings and rings. I expect it will go to voicemail. I'm even less prepared to leave a message. I want to hang up, but I let it ring. Suddenly, the line goes dead. Did I dial the right number? Did Stefan reject the call?

I jump as I hear Julian close behind, chuckling. "Your

wolf got what he wanted. Now it seems he's done with you."

Stefan doesn't think like that, does he? I've hurt him, that's all. In time I will find a way to make him understand and forgive me. I hang up the phone and Julian leads me back to the table. He seems to enjoy grabbing my waist and steering me around. He's truly from a different time. Apparently, fine ladies were once so frail they needed help to get to the table. What a lovely era for women.

As I arrive at my seat, I see that Julian hasn't cleaned off my chair. I use my hand to wipe off a layer of dust and immediately start to sneeze. Julian produces a handkerchief from somewhere, and I wipe my nose as I try to sit in a dress that wasn't made for sitting. "I need to go wash my hands."

Julian frowns as his tosses a napkin at me. "Just wipe your fingers and eat."

Wipe and eat. How sanitary.

I clean off my hands as best I can, then warily take the crystal goblet and smell the red liquid. Thankfully, it's only wine. Julian lifts the silver lid covering my plate. I expect something gruesome to be revealed, like a human heart, but it's a small bag of chips and a packaged snack cake. What a luxurious meal. The best thing about it is the plate: bone china with a painted black rose.

Julian sits in the shadows across from me, watching smugly as I devour the chips. I wonder if he is intentionally feeding me unhealthy food. He isn't eating anything. Am I his main course? I need to know more about how this works. "Can you eat regular food?"

"We can eat and excrete the same foods as you, though

my tastes are quite different."

"Then why do you need blood?"

"Blood provides a type of nutrition that food cannot, and it feeds our powers."

"But do you have to hurt people to get it? Can't you start a blood bank or something? Or use animal blood?"

Julian huffs, his patience thinning. "It's not just the blood. We also take a portion of the soul. So it needs to be a living human."

"You suck souls?? What does that do to people?"

Julian smiles. Never a good sign. "You're certainly the curious one. Well, never fear, all will be answered. Tomorrow I'll take you hunting."

What?? Does he expect me to drink blood? "Why do you want me with you?"

"It's easier to acquire prey with a beautiful woman at my side."

Just the sort of compliment that every girl wants to hear. "I won't help you hurt someone."

"Who says I hurt them? They enjoy every moment and beg me for more."

I want nothing to do with this. But I'm tired and it doesn't seem smart to get into an argument with him. "Thank you for lunch. I'd like to take a nap now."

Julian waves, dismissing me from the table. "As you like, but this evening I'll call on you for the hunt."

I make a noncommittal sound and leave the long table.

I lie on Cassandra's soft bed, feeling lightheaded from guzzling the wine. It feels good to be in a room of my own, away from Julian. It's only the middle of the day, but I'm so sleepy, and I feel myself drifting into Cassandra's dream world.

Julian plans to torment me. I know this. But it will be worth it if he gives up Síndóm to save Kaya. Can I trust him to do that? Maybe not. The weapon makes him nervous. He'll be reluctant to hand it over.

My only hope is to resurrect the feelings he once had for Cassandra. Back then, he would have done anything for her. But he doesn't feel that way about me. Can I awaken those feelings in him without getting emotionally involved? It's a dangerous gambit. I hate him, and if I ever stop hating him, I will have become a monster.

Sleep draws me to Cassandra, a welcome diversion from what is to come.

Lair of the Bears

STEFAN HILDEBRAND

I THROW MY cell phone into the gas station's garbage can. If I keep it I'll be tempted to call Emma. I need to stay away from her. That's the smart move.

After I finish filling my tank, I grab my sharpest knife and enter a filthy restroom to do something I should have done a long time ago.

I stand in front of the cracked bathroom mirror, using the knife to shave my head. It does a surprisingly good job, but I don't like myself bald.

I run my hand over my scalp. The tattoo is still there, of course, right on top of my head: a snarling wolf, with red eyes made from ink mixed with real wolf's blood.

I swallow a sudden wave of emotion. For the first time in nearly ten years, I'm not hiding who I am.

As I leave the bathroom, I toss my roll of wintergreen antacids into the trash.

In the rolling hills of northern Maine, I finally reach the tiny town of Trenson. I'm not sure what you need to qualify as an actual town, but I'm pretty sure Trenson doesn't have it. It's just a string of isolated shacks built of bleached wood and rusted steel.

Clan Trenson runs the copper mine here. Normals are not allowed. As I drive through, I see one of the bear-folk, a woman with hard eyes hanging laundry on an outdoor line. She looks like she could bench-press a car.

A young boy in the street squats near a huge pothole filled with water. He's made a boat from an empty beer can. His eyes widen in surprise as I drive around him, as if he's never seen a car on this street. Can you even call it a street when there's more dirt than pavement?

I don't see any security, but I'm sure they know I'm here. Bears can smell a stranger in town, especially a wolf.

I don't know where to go. I can't see any public buildings, so I decide to head for the mine.

I park my car in a gravel lot at the top of a hill next to town. The open mine is a dizzying sight. It looks like God twisted a giant screw out of the ground, leaving behind a huge, spiraling pit to hell. I see insects crawling along the swirled ledges and realize they are men.

An enormous bearded guy sits at a nearby checkpoint. He gives me the stink-eye as he slurps soup from a thermos. A stray noodle squirms in his beard like a pale worm.

I tilt my shaved head toward him, showing my wolf tattoo.

He spits, reaches for an old handheld radio, and clicks the "send" button three times, a universal signal for help.

Giant shifters begin to pour from the mine. They emerge in human form with pickaxes and sledgehammers that look like small toys in their enormous hands. *Any one of them could crush me like a bug, and there are dozens. Was coming here my last mistake?*

An older man with a coffee-stained clipboard emerges from the crowd. He steps closer, pulling on his salt-and-pepper beard as he takes a long whiff of me and speaks in a tone of disgust. "Hello, wolf."

I try to look calm. "Hello, bear."

"Your people never arranged safe passage."

"They don't know I'm here."

He raises a bushy eyebrow and turns back to his crew. "Who wants the kill?"

A dozen hands go up. I picture myself with a pickax in my gut. Bears don't like to kill you quick. Time to say something … anything. "I just shot a Knight of Rome. She's dead and I'm looking for a place to lie low."

Their leader's gray eyes grow narrow. "Why'd you shoot her?"

"She seemed to need it."

The corners of his lips curl in a half-smile. *Maybe I'll get a quick death after all.* He spits before speaking. "Why didn't you go to Corby?"

"Because I pissed them off."

"Any chance KoR followed you here?"

"I don't make those kinds of mistakes."

He digs his dirty fingernails into his beard as he thinks. After a moment, he comes to a decision and speaks to his men. "We'll give him a run of the lair."

Some of the men look disappointed, some look pleased. *What the hell is a 'run of the lair'? Nothing good, I'm sure.*

A gang of big men pulls me into a plywood shack built into the side of a hill about a mile from the mine. They strip me of my weapons and clothes and shove them in one of the old wooden cubbyholes that line the walls. I notice several dozen sets of clothes stuffed into other slots, most of them collecting dust. *Why have these clothes gone unclaimed? Maybe the owners are dead.*

The bear leader points to a door at the back of the shack. "Walk through the lair. If you make it to the other side, we'll talk."

If? But this is no time to show hesitation. I open the door to find a tunnel leading down into the darkness. A soft, wet breeze rises from the shadows, carrying the scent of death. I get a mental image of a huge bear down there, a hungry bear waiting for its next meal.

I invoke my wolf and stroll casually into the tunnel. As I leave the shack behind, my nose warns me of what lies ahead. I don't smell any animals here, only people, and some of them are dead. This isn't a mine shaft—it's something else entirely.

Sharp stones prick my feet as I continue to descend, but my wolf absorbs the damage and I do not bleed. I can smell something else now, cooked meat. It makes my mouth water.

As I round a bend in the tunnel, I see a flickering candle ahead and someone sitting in a chair. As I get closer I can make out an old woman with a bloody ax in her lap. I can tell from her scent that she's a bear. She glances up from the bone she's gnawing on, unfazed by my wolfish appearance. With a quick gesture of annoyance, she points to a thick iron door behind her. What lies beyond that door? Is she sending me to my doom? I don't smell a threat on her, but I keep one eye on her ax as I push open the door on shrieking hinges.

I pass into a candlelit kitchen that looks straight out of the Middle Ages. Not a single electric appliance in sight. Another old woman hunches over a wood stove. She looks exactly like the woman outside. She stirs a big iron pot with a wooden spoon. It smells like some sort of stew. On a bloody bench beside her I see a filleted human leg. My stomach turns as I realize the delicious smell is human flesh. Most shifters, including my own clan, avoid human meat. But Trenson is an exception.

I glance behind me, and the woman with the ax stands there with a toothless grin. Damn, she moves quiet. I immediately work out a strategy for fighting the twin women, though if they invoke their bears my chances are not good.

The woman with the ax points to an opening at the back of the kitchen. Moving forward is good. This is not a place I want to stay. I edge sideways toward the opening, keeping an eye on both of them. They may be old, but something tells me they can still move fast in a fight.

I enter a short passage and emerge into a small room dominated by some sort of huge antique weaving contraption. A third old woman, identical to the others, sits behind the machine, loading it with a combination of red and white thread. She isn't an ax-wielding cannibal, but for some reason, she worries me most of all.

I survey the candlelit room and find a bucket of blood and a table scattered with drying red wool. The two other women stand behind me now, grinning and carrying axes, but neither shows an intent to harm. They pass by me and join the third woman, hovering at the end of the weaving machine.

The female trio examines a length of woven cloth that has emerged from the device. Shit, I know who these women are! When I was a kid in Corby, Ms. Lystad taught us about the Norns, the three völva who spin the threads of fate. They are supposed to be a myth, but obviously they're real, and working for the bears.

I suddenly feel very small and insignificant. And I fear for the future of my clan.

As the women study the red-and-white cloth, they begin to cackle. Are they reading my fate? Why do they find it so hilarious? I can't keep quiet any longer. "What do you see?"

They frown at me. Apparently, speaking is a breach of protocol. One of them points her ax at a doorway behind the contraption. "Begone, wolf."

They don't have to tell me twice.

I emerge in a wooded area on the other side of the tunnel and uninvoke, unsure of what awaits me. The group of armed men approaches, looking surprised to see me. Their leader steps forth and speaks to me. "Name's Storlie." He doesn't offer his hand.

Weird introducing myself without clothes. "I'm Stefan Hildebrand. What the hell was that about?"

His eyes drift away for a moment. "I remember that name. While back. You were some sort of fighter."

"TKD."

He scoffs. "That's for pussies. You should do *Lausatök.*"

I remain silent, knowing not to talk about Lausatök around bears. Here it's not just a traditional Norse martial art, it's a religion.

The men load me roughly into the back of Storlie's beat-up pickup truck. He drives me around the mountain and we pick up my clothes back at the shack. I get dressed and Storlie drives me into town. He pulls up in front of some sort of community center hidden in the trees. It's a ramshackle two-story building that looks like a hunting lodge built a hundred years ago.

Storlie and I exit the truck and approach the building. Three wolf/dog half-breeds sit outside the building. One of them is licking his balls. The dogs growl at the sight of me, straining against their long chains. Storlie grins. I understand the insinuation. He's showing that werebears are masters of the werewolves. But that's not true. Bears are great in a fight but will never be masters of anything until they get organized and start working together.

As we enter the old building, the smell of bacon gets my mouth watering. A group of surprised miners sitting at a long table looks up from their food as we enter. Storlie turns to me and points to a flight of stairs. "There's a fellow up there who'll want to hear about that Knight you shot. Second floor, first room on the right. Don't open the drapes, he don't like the light. Afterwards, come down and eat if you like."

Not sure of the protocol here, I tap softly on the outside of the wooden door. After a few moments, a tired voice responds from within. "For the love of God, what time is it?"

It can't be much past 5:00 p.m. Is this man sick in bed? I crack the door open and peer into the shadows. "Storlie sent me to talk to you."

The voice sounds a little annoyed now. "About what?"

As my eyes adjust, I see a man lying on the lower shelf of a bunk bed. I can tell from his smell that he's a vampire. What the hell is a vampire doing in Were country? Best to just to lay my cards on the table. "I shot a Knight of Rome. Storlie thought you'd want to hear about it."

"What??" He swings his legs over the bed and pushes himself into a sitting position. It's impossible to tell how old vampires are, but in the dim light I see a man in his midthirties with a big square jaw and the face of a leader. But his strong body doesn't match his beaten-down voice. "Who are you?"

"Stefan Hildebrand from Clan Corby. I've been under-cover in KoR for the last nine years. Who are you?"

He nods and extends a strong hand. "Lord Lorance Sparkes, Ruler of the North American Realm of the Black Rose Society."

Vampire nobility! "What's a vam…Transcendent…doing in Trenson?"

He sighs. "I find myself asking that very question." He points to a rough wooden chair in the corner of the room. I sit and remain silent.

He stretches and cracks his neck, finally speaking. "Have you heard of *Vera Gentis?*"

I shake my head.

He gets to his feet and adjusts the drapes to keep out the light. "As you know, both of our tribes consider the word *paranormal* to be derogatory. And yet we do need a term to distinguish us from the humans. So we have named ourselves Vera Gentis, the true people. We are an organization building a cross-cultural resistance to the Knights."

Vampires and were working together? Good luck with that. "Have you pitched this to Corby?"

He slumps a little. "I did, but they claim to be following their own approach against KoR." He straightens and turns suddenly. "Wait, is that you? You're their approach?"

"Yeah, but it didn't work out so good."

"How were you discovered?"

"I wasn't. They sent me to kill an innocent girl just because she was a Transcendent in a past life. I couldn't take that kind of shit anymore. So I left."

"Hmmm, what girl?"

"Emma Rue."

"That's her past life name?"

"No, she was called … I don't know. She told me but I forget. Melissa Cook? Melissa Cross?"

His voice comes to life. "Cassandra Cross?"

"That's it."

In a flash he's on me, lifting me from the chair with impossibly strong arms. I nearly invoke, but I don't smell a threat. His voice sounds alive and eager. "Cassandra Cross, from Newport, Rhode Island?"

I nod. "You knew her?"

He pats me warmly on the shoulder, his voice filled with excitement. "This is joyous news! Cassandra is a remarkable woman. She was once the heir to my former governorship. We have to find her at once."

"Well, see, I'm not really up for that."

Lorance doesn't look pleased. Shit, I don't want to fight another vampire.

SEPULCHER

CASSANDRA CROSS

1814

EMMA'S PAST LIFE

AS WE DINE on the deck of the *HMS Tonnant*, we try to ignore the explosions in the distance. This eighty-gun ship of the line currently stands in quiet water, a distant observer to the slaughter taking place across the channel in Baltimore. I take a spoonful of carrot pudding into my mouth but my fear has rendered it tasteless. Each burst of fire in the battle beyond tears at my heart. I can do nothing but wait for the explosion that will end Tom's life.

Julian sits at the table beside me, along with Mr. Key, a wonderful abolitionist lawyer, and Colonel Skinner, a dogged prisoner exchange agent. Across the table sits the esteemed British Vice Admiral Cochrane and his stern Rear Admiral Cockburn.

This is our third dinner on the *Tonnant*. We've been forced to remain aboard until the bombardment of Fort

McHenry is complete. Julian and I could escape at any time, of course, but we are loath to leave without our friend, the aging Dr. William Beanes, being held in the brig below. Though mortal, Dr. Beanes has proven friendly to our community, one of the few researching the afflictions of our kind. Among other things, he has developed a salve that greatly reduces burns caused by overexposure to the sun.

I can no longer tolerate the strained dinner conversation. I excuse myself and retire to the railing to watch the unrelenting artillery assault.

Julian, ever sensitive to my moods, joins me with a gentle embrace. "Does Tom still live?"

I look out at the fort's ramparts. An explosion lights up the American flag. How can it still be flying? And how can Tom possibly survive this rain of fire? I think of him, concentrating on his soul. I see nothing, feel nothing. I blink away tears and hug Julian. "I think he's gone."

Julian strokes my hair and it helps to ease the pain.

Poor Tom. I have not seen him since that night in the ballroom pantry, some thirty-three years ago. But we have exchanged correspondence on occasion. His life has been nothing but misery since I abandoned him for Julian. His second wife died childless and he found himself alone in the world, all of his family gone. He once said that my letters were the only thing keeping him from madness. I would like to have visited him, but seeing me still in my youth would invite too many uncomfortable questions.

I tried to convince Tom not to re-enlist, but he was

determined to do it and the United States Army was eager to bring back their few remaining leaders from the first war, despite their advanced age. He sent me a letter before he went to Baltimore. It said simply ...*Men such as me do not die of old age.*

What a brave, foolish man. I hug Julian tighter, squeezing some comfort from him. "I'd like to commission a sepulcher on our property, something worthy of him."

"Of course, my love, whatever you wish."

Mr. Key, unaware of my sadness, ambles up to the railing with a smile and peers out at the fort. "Remarkable. Our flag is still there!"

A cool breeze blows in from over the water, bringing the acrid scent of gunpowder. I know that Tom's soul flies free upon that wind of war.

I watch the sweating workmen depart the grounds, signaling the end of construction on the sepulcher behind Refuge d'Amoureux. Julian's odd fascination with the project took me by surprise. It's not that he's gleeful about the death of a rival, more that he's intrigued by the specter of death and the mystery of reincarnation. Some years ago, I operated a literary salon in Boston for female Transcendent, but it was impossible to keep Julian away. And whenever he joined us, the conversation inevitably turned to death.

The Transcendent are not the dead things from the folktales. We feel pain, and we bleed, but our bodies are more

resilient than those of mortals. We can only die from cata-
strophic injuries such as beheading or prolonged exposure
to fire. Surprisingly, the Knights kill very few of our number. Most of us die at our own hands, taken by heartsick-
ness. Our kind is prone to melancholy and no one knows
why.

Julian, a rebel in our community, believes that our long
lives defy the natural order, so we have an innate drive to
restore the balance by either ending ourselves or elevating
all mortals. Needless to say, that is the sort of talk that's
prevented him from reaching a leadership position in the
Black Rose Society. Artists such as he have a reputation for
being heretical. But of course, that's one of the many reasons I love him.

Barely able to contain his excitement over the comple-
tion of his project, Julian takes my hand and leads me to
the sepulcher. He hasn't allowed me inside since construction began, determined to surprise me with its design.

Two stone angels, their faces defiant, fiercely defend the
entrance of the low stone building. I see no way of opening
the heavy stone door. I brush my fingers against the stone,
engraved with a relief of an explosion over Fort McHenry.

Julian grins. "Don't trouble yourself. That's not a real
door. It's there to thwart grave robbers."

"Who would want to rob it?"

Julian shrugs. "I've no idea."

He leads me behind the building. "We'll need to jump."
He surprises me by leaping straight up onto the roof of the

structure, a leap impossible for a mortal. Though not as athletic as Julian, I manage to make the jump without creating a scandal of my yellow embroidered silk dress.

On the roof stands a series of low stone pedestals arranged in a circle. As he sits on one, it sinks with an audible click. "The secret is to make a 'C,' for Cassandra." He hops excitedly from one pedestal to the next, putting his weight on each in a pattern that marks out a "C." The disk of stone in the circle between the pedestals slides smoothly back, revealing a set of stone stairs that lead down into darkness.

I offer him my praise. "Truly the *pièce de résistance.*" But try as I might, I can't share his morbid enthusiasm.

Hand in hand, we descend into the bowels of the sepulcher. It seems larger inside than on the outside. Part of it must be below ground.

As we reach the floor of the crypt, I am stunned to see three elaborate sarcophagi, two of them open and one closed. Each of the massive stone coffins is guarded by a statue of its owner.

Julian leads me to the closed sarcophagus. "I took the liberty of having his body transferred from Baltimore, so he would already be here for you." At the foot of the sarcophagus, a younger version of Tom stands tall, carved in marble and looking *très galant.* The likeness is uncanny.

I try to get some sense of Tom beneath the heavy stone lid. But nothing is there, only his bones. I wonder where his soul has gone. I hope it has found a happier life.

I turn to the nearby sarcophagi that Julian has prepared

for our eventual end. They lie open, waiting like hungry mouths. Julian's statue, standing tall nearby, is powerfully cut, his loving gaze fixed on my statue, flattering and life-like. My statue's eyes are turned toward Tom, but its neck to Julian.

I notice that Julian has not made a place for Angelo. His Maker disappeared when I transcended and has not been seen since. From time to time, Angelo sends a letter from London, and they always put Julian in a foul mood. Their rivalry over me appeals to my small-minded side. It assures me that Julian still cares, that he will always care. And should fate take our lives, our bodies will remain together in this sepulcher while our souls take flight, seeking each other throughout eternity. I kiss Julian on the cheek. "It's a lovely resting place, thank you."

Will he and I sleep here together a hundred years from now? Two hundred? Will someone from the distant future one day enter this crypt, run their fingers over this beautifully sculpted sarcophagus and wonder who I was? It's a pity the dead can't speak, for I would have a story to tell.

BLISS

EMMA RUE

THE PRESENT

I RISE FROM Cassandra's bed, still feeling her grief over Tom's death. Visions of the darkly beautiful sepulcher swim in my head.

I look through the window at the dying sun, remembering that Julian has made plans for us to "hunt." What horrors will this night bring?

As I turn, I find Julian standing behind me. My heart pounds as I stumble back against the window. I want to yell at him. Hasn't he ever heard of knocking? But I need to play it smart and stick with the plan of reawakening his feelings for Cassandra. "Julian, I've been thinking. It's okay for you to call me Cassandra. I want us to be like we were in the old times." I watch his face for a reaction.

He throws an item of clothing into my arms. "Dress for the hunt."

I examine the dress, a tight black micromini with body-baring slashes. He must have stolen it from a porn star. "I told you, I'm not helping you hurt someone. And I'm not comfortable wearing this."

Julian slowly approaches, voice whispering like the rustle of silk. "The first time is always difficult. But I can help you."

He's radiating those pheromones again. That rich and intimate scent that makes my whole body quiver. He must be able to turn it off and on at will. The dress falls from my hands. I feel like I'm dreaming. I see a waterfall breaking on a bed of mossy rocks, then a wildfire swirling through a forest of skeletal trees. He's talking now. I must try to listen.

"...It makes everything more pleasant. We call it *bliss*."

Bliss. It was in Cassandra's memories. Some sort of drug released by a vampire's bite.

Suddenly I'm hanging in Julian's arms as he carries me to the bed. He lays me down gently and rolls my head back, exposing my neck. Is he going to bite me?

I'm not ready. This is all happening too fast. In my mind, I'm running from the room. But my body remains on the bed, eager for his attention.

I feel his cold, immortal breath on my throat. "Take my thorns, girl."

I cry out in pain as his pale fangs slip into my flesh.

And then the bliss hits.

Every nerve of my body explodes in ecstasy. Every muscle clenches in a sweet, glorious spasm. I open my mouth to scream but can't make a sound. I've never experienced anything so intensely powerful.

I fear that I will never feel this rapture again, and I begin to weep.

His soft words caress my ear. "I know the secret of ultimate pleasure. Shall I share it with you?"

I nod behind a wall of tears, hanging on his every word.

"You will never feel more alive than when you surrender your soul to me."

I find myself on the crowded floor of a posh beachside dance club. Hot, colored lights pulse through my skin as darkly powerful music hums through my bones. My body writhes in the slashed micromini, showing off incredibly sexy dance moves I didn't know I had.

Julian dances across from me, wearing tight black pants with a green brocade vest. He takes my hands and leads me into a strange dance that reminds me of Cassandra's cotillion, only with grinding hips and tremendous speed. How am I keeping up? I am his willing puppet, joyfully anticipating the tug of each string.

As the crowd parts around us to watch the spectacle, I find myself growing dizzy. The pulsing music slows to a dull roar. The colored lights fade to black and white. Darkness begins to swallow the room. I hear my heart pounding like a drum, louder and faster, threatening to explode.

I awake in Julian's arms. He sits at the bar with me in his lap, holding a cold glass of water to my mouth. "You've exceeded your body's limits. You must drink and rest."

I suck the water into my mouth. It feels like liquid light, flowing slowly down to my toes. Almost immediately it gives me strength. I sit up, now able to hold the glass on my own. I become more aware of my surroundings and quickly adjust the slashes of my dress to reveal less of my breasts.

This end of the bar is crowded with beautiful women. Half of them watch Julian with lust in their eyes, and the other half glare at me, as if willing me to die. I've never been the focus of so much jealousy. It feels ... amazing.

Julian whispers into my ear. "Choose, my gem, one lucky woman to bring home to Elizabeth."

Elizabeth? I could ask him about her, but he wouldn't answer. I try to channel Cassandra's power into my weakened body. "I will choose for you, but *only* if she doesn't get hurt."

His voice feels like a cool embrace. "Of course. For you, anything."

Are his feelings for Cassandra finally returning? Probably too much to hope for.

I survey the women who don't want to scratch my eyes out. There are three of them: a girl with short dark hair and perfect skin, another with huge green eyes and twice my cleavage, and a third with pale features and long honey-colored hair.

I can't decide. It's like trying to choose a puppy. I feel a stab of guilt at that thought. These are women, not puppies, and I am about to set a monster on them. "I can't do it, Julian. Coming heah was a bad idea. *Here.*"

He leans in, his ruby lips nuzzling my neck. I fall limp into his arms, his force of will dominating me.

Through lidded eyes, I look into the souls of the women. The long-haired girl is not a nice person. I find myself whispering to Julian, "The one with the long hair. Don't hurt her."

Foot Rub

CYNTHIA GREENE

I DRINK A DEL'S as a nervous tailor cuffs my pants. I can barely taste the normally delicious lemonade on Fragface's dead tongue.

I have a few hours to pass before Kaya and Seble return home from school, and I'm tired of looking like a hobo. I've come to this strip-mall menswear shop and selected a gray three-piece suit with white pinstripes, a white shirt, and a burgundy tie. I think it civilizes Fragface, a little anyway. A man in a suit gets respect. I'll tell people I'm a wealthy investor who received these horrible facial scars when my Mercedes crashed.

A bead of sweat drops from the tailor's nose. "All done, sir. You can pick this up tomorrow."

He can hardly wait to get me out of his shop. I loom over him. "I need it *now.*"

"But, sir…" He trails off, wilting under the glare from my jigsaw face. "Yes sir. I can have it done in fifteen minutes."

I step out of the pants and he tries not to look at the scars on my pale, muscular legs. "I want a hat too."

"Of course, sir, anything you like."

Men don't wear hats anymore, but they really should.

I realize my outfit is still missing one accessory. A gun. Just the thought of a gun makes Fragface's calloused fingers twitch. He and guns are old friends. But without a proper I.D., I can't buy a weapon.

Fortunately, I know someone who owns a sawed-off shotgun. And I know where he keeps it.

I shove my fist through the glass window in the back door of Bill's house, a two-story colonial in the heart of Elmhurst. Reaching inside, I open the door, enter the kitchen, and hurry to punch the code into his home alarm. Bill is at work, the twins in school, and the Heifer is at yoga, so I have the place to myself.

I've done a lot of walking in these new shoes and my feet hurt. That surprises me, because the rest of my body is numb. I had hoped that Fragface felt no pain, but no such luck.

I walk through the most poorly kept home I can imagine. If Heifer stopped wasting her time on futile attempts to improve her body, perhaps this place would become livable. Surely Bill must have realized by now that he chose the wrong wife.

I go into the bedroom and retrieve the sawed-off shotgun from under the bed. It has a trigger lock, but I know where

Bill hides the key. I fetch it from a painfully tacky fabric-lined dresser drawer and unlock the weapon. Fragface's greedy hands take over, doing all sorts of impressive gun things. The man was clearly a wizard with firearms. I take it that the weapon is now ready to fire. I tuck it out of sight, clutching it under the arm of my suit jacket. Now I'm a proper thug.

My toes are really hurting as I return to the kitchen. I sit at the table, take off my black leather oxfords and rub my feet. I remove my wool socks and discover the problem. My feet have turned green. In places, dead skin is sliding off the bone. How disappointing. It seems this body came with a shelf life.

I hear a noise out in the living room. No one should be here! I grab the shotgun just as Heifer walks into the kitchen and drops her yoga mat on the table. My rumbling voice scares her half to death. "I thought you were still at yoga."

She squeals like a slaughtered pig when she sees my fragmented face.

I point the shotgun at her. "Shut up, or I'll give you another hole to scream out of." *What an intimidating threat. I would have made an excellent criminal!*

Nearly hyperventilating, she manages to speak. "Who are you? What do you want?"

I only came for the gun, but now I find myself wanting more. "I want you to rub my feet."

"What?"

"You heard me."

I sit at the table, the shotgun pointed at her, and extend a rotting foot.

Horrified, she desperately scrambles around in her purse. "I have money! You can have everything, just put down the gun!"

My roar rattles the kitchen. "Rub. My. Feet!"

"Okay, okay!" Crying, she scrambles to her knees. Her eyes widen in horror as she stares at my decaying feet. With trembling hands, she touches them gingerly, as if they're about to bite. She gags as she begins to rub.

I believe this is the most fun I have ever had. "I have some questions for you, Heifer." She's so scared she doesn't seem to hear me. I grab her hair and shake her head. "Are you listening?"

"Yes, whatever you want! Just don't hurt me. I have two kids!"

Bitch. Those should have been my children. "Does Bill ever talk about the first love of his life?" *She looks confused. Does she think she's his first love? Hah!* "Think, Heifer! It was before he met you, a woman named Cynthia Greene."

"Oh yes, he told me about her. What's she got to do with anything?"

"What did he say? Tell me *exactly* what he said."

She hesitates. I raise my hand to strike her and she blurts it all out. "She was crazy, the worst mistake he ever made. She ended up in prison for killing all those mothers she thought were abusive. Then she hung herself."

Crazy? I have the strongest urge to blow her cow head off. But the kids will be home soon, and I need her to look after them until I can get a proper body and finally take her place.

I feel a sudden pain, and Heifer screams. One of my rotting toes has broken off in her hand. "Oh my God!" She drops the toe and scrambles away from it.

I look at the piece of myself lying on the kitchen floor. What a disgusting spectacle. How shall I punish the cow for her clumsiness? Suddenly, a lovely idea occurs to me. I pick up the lost toe and put it in the garbage disposal. This will certainly upset her. Who wants that mess in their sink?

I hit the switch and hear the bone bouncing against the disposal blade. Eventually, the blade captures the toe and grinds it down to nothing.

Heifer vomits, looking more miserable than I have ever seen her. The garbage disposal was a stroke of genius. I'm so very pleased with myself!

I put my shoes and socks back on as Heifer sobs in the corner of the kitchen. Then I grab her hair and pull her up. "This is your to-do list. First, I want you to dust the top of your refrigerator. It's filthy. Tall people can see up there, you know." I point deeper into the house. "Then you've got messes in the bathroom and bedroom to clean."

❧♡❧

Heifer has a nice car, a luxury SUV with seat warmers. I drive away from Bill's house with a smile on my jigsaw face.

That cow has hours of housework ahead of her. I told her I would be outside, spying on her through the windows in case she tried to make a call.

Fragface is a good driver, but working the pedals hurts my decomposing feet.

Kaya and Seble will be out of school soon. I should arrive there just before they get home. Then I can use Kaya to get to Emma.

INTO THE GRAVE

CASSANDRA CROSS

1788

EMMA'S PAST LIFE

I STAND KNEE-DEEP in snow as I watch the pallbearers carry my father into the burying grounds. Their cold breaths rise like steam above the hardwood coffin.

No one could tell me why Father died. One moment he was here, and the next he was snatched away by the hands of fate. Mother was sharing a meal of chowder and johnny-cakes with him, so at least he did not die alone.

In those brief, terrible moments when I sometimes imagined how he would die, it was always lying in bed, with me sitting vigil at his side. He would tell me a war story, imparting some sort of wisdom, and then touch me on the nose in the same comforting way he had done since I was an infant.

Mother, cloaked in a black veil, stands shivering between my aunt and uncle, each supporting her by an arm. She and I rarely speak anymore. Last night she told me, with an edge to her voice, that I haven't aged a day since divorcing Tom. She has never forgiven me for abandoning him, and is increasingly bitter and suspicious about my persistent youth.

Julian is in Europe on business, so I must face this funeral without my beloved at my side. Lorance stands with me in Julian's place, and nearby are my friends, Hope Fenwick and nearly every Black Rose from the region. The men wear black hatbands as favors and the women carry black handkerchiefs. Both the hatbands and handkerchiefs are embroidered with a black rose made of blaze-dyed thread. To Transcendent eyes, it looks as if the petals are pulsing with veins of blood. It wasn't until today that I realized how much these people care for me. Under Lorance's tutelage, I have worked to strengthen and extend our organization, and it seems my efforts have not been wasted.

Across from me stands General Washington, in full uniform with his blue wool coat with the gilded buttons. It was so good of him to come. Last night, while the mourners gorged on food and wine, the General took me aside and told me how important my father had been to the cause of freedom. How touched and honored I felt to have the great General share his thoughts with me. There is talk that the Confederation Congress will make him the president of a new nation if the Constitution is ratified, a well-deserved honor that may never come to pass. Rhode Island has refused to ratify because it would require them to drop their worthless state currency. We may be free states, but we are anything but united.

Flakes of snow drift onto my black headdress and remain there, unmelting. Beneath my long black cloak I wear a black silk gown. My hands are adorned by my heart-blaze ring and a piece of mourning jewelry, a ring with a damascened band and an oval portrait of Father painted on ivory. Everywhere at this gathering, there is black, as if a flock of crows had landed on this snow-covered ground. And the irony is, Father hated black.

The pallbearers lower him into the ground without a eulogy. That, at least, was how he would have wanted it. I see that General Washington is frowning. It seems the grave was not dug wide enough all the way to the bottom, and they are unable to lower the casket completely inside. Many in the uncomfortable crowd avert their gaze as the casket is hauled back up.

Before anyone else can react, General Washington finds a shovel and leaps into the hole, an impressive act for a man of his years. A casket-bearer finds another shovel and joins him in widening the grave.

I whisper to Lorance in the True Tongue, "My father always complained that in war, nothing proceeds according to plan. He would have had a chuckle over this."

Lorance nods. "No doubt, my dear, no doubt."

A flock of dappled gulls flies over, the cold air somehow sharpening their cries.

Mother begins to wail. "Whatever our differences, I pity her. The Transcendent know that a soul will return. We recognize familiar souls when we see them again. But the mortal enjoy no such comfort."

Lorance turns to me. "Your father may have *already* returned, perhaps to this area. Will you search for him?"

"I think not. It seems … inappropriate … somehow."

"Ah yes, I think I understand. May I ask you another question?"

"Of course."

"When I die, will you seek out *my* next incarnation?"

"If you wish it."

"Please do. I will endeavor not to return as a boor."

I smile despite the grim occasion. "How lovely if we could actually choose our next existence."

Lorance nods. "How lovely if we could remember our lives past, if we could remember the mistakes we've made. If only I could pass a letter on to my next self, detailing all the lessons I've learned."

"That would make a brilliant salon project. We could each write a letter of advice to our future selves."

"And what would your advice be?"

I am struck mute by his question. Having broken Tom's heart and hardened my mother's, I am in no position to give advice. How exactly did these disasters come to pass?

I think back on the moment that Father told me of Tom's intentions. If I had refused the marriage, it would have hurt Father, but not nearly as much as the scandalous divorce that followed. Appeasement and compromise have ended in sorrow. If you remember anything about me, future self, remember this—trust your instincts and follow them, regardless of the cost, for there will be a far greater price to pay if you do not.

Elizabeth Immortal

EMMA RUE

THE PRESENT

I WAKE UP on Cassandra's bed and think about the lesson she wanted to impart. Have I been brave enough to trust my instincts? Or have I been making compromises that I'll eventually have to pay for? I am nineteen years old. I know there are many things I don't yet understand about the world. But with Cassandra's wisdom, perhaps I can survive this.

I slide off the bed and stand on wobbly legs. Why does my body ache like this? I see that I'm wearing the black micromini and it all comes back. The dance club. The girl with the long hair. And something else, hovering at the edge of a blurry memory. Julian bit me!

As I change into the pale green gown, I look out the window and see bright moonlight on the brambles. How much time has passed? My trembling hands light a candle and I approach the vanity, afraid to look at my reflection. Has Julian's bite transformed me into a monster?

I raise the candle and examine myself in the gilded mirror. My face looks normal. The two small holes where his "thorns" found my neck are painless and nearly invisible, with only some light bruising around them.

Julian told me that I could not become a vampire, and it seems he's right. I haven't transformed. But still, I don't feel the same. *Something* has definitely happened. Am I his slave now? Did he suck away my soul? And what did he do to that poor girl with the long hair? I shouldn't have gone with him to the club. I wouldn't have gone if he hadn't drugged me. That bliss is powerful stuff. If it was sold on the open market it would destroy civilization.

A knock on the door startles me. Since when does Julian knock? Or has Stefan returned? "Come in."

I'm disappointed to see Julian enter. His feet are bare and he's wearing a burgundy robe, casually open to reveal his muscular torso. It's an erotic and unsettling sight. He smiles at me. "How are you feeling?"

How lovely that he cares so much for my well-being. "What happened to the girl from the club, the one with the long hair? Did you hurt her?"

"Did I hurt *you?*"

I touch the wound on my neck. I can barely feel it. "What's going to happen to me because of this bite?"

"Ah, you're worried you'll turn into a bat at any moment. Well, rest assured, that won't happen."

"Did you … take any of my soul?"

"A bit. That's what we do."

I feel sick inside. Tears spring to my eyes. "Will it …
grow back?"

Julian laughs loud and long.

A sudden anger overwhelms me and I step forward to
slap him. But he isn't there. I turn to find him behind me,
grinning. He has circled around me in Velox.

He speaks slowly, as if to a child. "It doesn't 'grow back.'
The part I took belongs to me now, and there's no way to
return it. But you needn't get hysterical. I would have to
feed on you several more times before any serious damage
was done."

He's standing very close now. I feel goose bumps spread
across my skin as I breathe in his supernatural scent. I know
I am angry with him, but suddenly I can't remember why.

He draws his long fingernail lightly across my cheek as
he circles me. "It's time for you to meet Elizabeth."

"She's here now?"

He smiles mysteriously. I can feel his cool breath on my
face. "She's always been here."

I have a sense of impending doom as Julian leads me into
his bedroom. I've never seen it in Cassandra's memories.
It has an ocean theme: a lush blue carpet woven with various gold sea creatures, and a huge wooden chest set at the
foot of a four-poster bed. The mother-of-pearl inlay in the
headboard depicts a seaside bacchanal. What the hell? I was
expecting a horrible dungeon, not some nouveau pirate's

den adorned with slutty mermaids.

I survey every corner of the room. Julian and I seem to be alone here.

He sits me down next to a wooden table that has some sort of old sea chart pressed under a pane of thick glass. His voice sounds strangely apologetic. "Before we begin, I must provide some context."

Begin what? I'm so nervous. My stomach is clenching.

"A century or so after your assassination, I gave up hope that you would ever return. I fell into a deep melancholy and spent most of my time in dormancy. Then, about six decades ago, a young couple moved into the mansion on the adjacent property, the lovely Elizabeth and her new husband, a man descended from old money."

And of course, being the gentleman that you are, you respected their marriage and left her alone.

Julian smiles as he speaks, every trace of his cruelty vanished. "Elizabeth and I began an exhilarating courtship. And for the first time in an age, I felt hope for the future."

Then the clouds return to his face. "We reached boldly for happiness. But we reached too far."

Julian dramatically lifts the lid of the giant wooden chest. He gestures for me to approach. Fear turns my legs to jelly as I push myself up from the table.

I glance fearfully into the chest and see a woman sleeping. A beautiful woman. A woman who looks a lot like Cassandra!

Julian sounds almost apologetic. "I'm not mad—I know she's not Cassandra. But the resemblance is striking, is it not? Fate must have brought her to my door."

Elizabeth lies atop a layer of dark silk cushions. She wears a vintage dress made of white lace and pale blue silk. She's lying too still, too perfectly posed to be sleeping. I look into her soul. She doesn't have one. "She's dead!"

"When we decided to advance our relationship, I attempted to elevate her. The transition is difficult on the mortal body. The sick or injured cannot survive it. And sometimes it claims even the healthy, as it did with Elizabeth."

I look at her perfectly preserved body. No foul smell, not one hair out of place. "Is she ... stuffed?"

"Don't be vulgar. I prefer to say I've immortalized her."

Julian carefully lifts her from the chest, her body rigid as a board. "Elizabeth, I'd like you to meet Cassandra."

Horror overwhelms me.

Before I realize it, I've fled the chamber and am racing down the stairs. I trip on the hem of my gown and nearly go sprawling.

My heart pounds as I run into Cassandra's room and throw the door shut, leaning against it in a hopeless attempt to prevent Julian's entry. Why didn't I run outside?

Julian has gone insane. These centuries of living here, obsessing over Cassandra, have driven him mad. I have to leave. It's only a matter of time before he gets around to having *me* stuffed.

Then I think of Kaya crying in the restaurant. I can't just leave her at the mercy of the creature that wants the dagger. But my plan to convince Julian to give me the dagger isn't going to work. I know this now.

If I can just survive one more day here, I'll wait until he's asleep, or until he goes out to feed, and then I'll tear this place apart until I find that dagger. Once I have it, I'll run and never look back.

Just one more day. For Kaya.

The Blót

STEFAN HILDEBRAND

I STILL CAN'T believe that I'm in my car, headed south on 95, going back to Providence to look for Emma. Lorance, a very persuasive man, sits hunched in the seat beside me, wearing sunglasses and a wide-brimmed hat tilted into the rising sun to protect his face.

Lorance's powerful voice sounds bright and cheerful. "You know, once we find Emma, I'd like you to consider taking a position in Vera Gentis."

"How'd you get me in the car? You use some of that vampire soul shit?"

Lorance sits in an incriminating silence as we pass around the Boston area. I see the exit for the 90 into Worcester. I've been meaning to check out the Arms and Armor collection at the Worcester Art Museum, but I've never had the time. It's just one more piece of life stolen from me by duty.

Lorance pulls his hat lower. "I'm not a warrior, Stefan. I'm a peacemaker, a community builder. We need a man who has studied the art of war, a man who knows the enemy. Master-at-Arms. That title has a ring to it, don't you think? Or would you prefer something more modern? Director of Field Operations?"

"I understand what you need. What about what *I* need?"

Lorance chuckles. "I can see your soul, my boy. I know what you need. You need to belong, to be accepted. We can offer you that. We can offer you a home. And then, of course, there's Cassandra, or Emma as you know her. We'll take her under our wing and you'll get to spend more time with her." He suppresses a smile.

Smug bastard. That's the trouble with vampires, always looking at your soul for the right strings to pull. This is going to be a long car ride.

Lorance and I search Emma's small apartment as her annoyed building manager waits outside. There's no sign that Emma's been here since my last visit, and no sign of the spirit that tried to enter me here. I find Emma's phone and replay the message from her friend, Melita.

Lorance, almost giddy, hurries around the apartment, running his hands over the huge collection of books. "This is most definitely Cassandra! The mark of her soul is every-where, particularly on the books."

This guy is *really* eager to find her. For some reason, that annoys me. "Did you and her have a thing?"

Lorance looks suddenly uncomfortable. "A ... what?"

"Were you sleeping with her?" *And the answer had better be no.*

Lorance sighs. "I have feelings for her, yes, but I only served as her mentor. She's the most gifted soulreader I've ever known."

I put down Emma's phone. "She has a friend, Melita. We should find her."

My fake FBI badge gets us through the door of Melita's apartment near an Italian neighborhood on Federal Hill. A pissed teenage girl named Seble glares at us. She doesn't like cops and speaks to us in an angry tone. "Mom's still at work. You'll have to come back."

Lorance stares intently at the back of the apartment. I can tell he's doing some sort of spooky vampire shit.

I use a commanding tone on Seble. "Who's in the back?"

Seble looks a little cowed. "Just Kaya. She's hiding."

I remember that name. She's the girl Emma mentioned. "We need to talk to her."

Seble shrugs. "Whatever, she's in Mom's room. Probably locked the door."

As Lorance and I walk down the narrow hallway, I catch a faint whiff of death. Something is very wrong here. Once out of Seble's eyeline, I invoke my wolf and draw a Knights of Rome .50-caliber handgun. Dim light reflects from the handle emblem, a gold laurel wreath on a crimson field.

Lorance points to a closed door and whispers to me. "Be careful—there are *two* people in there. And one of them is trouble."

Suddenly, a shotgun blast destroys the wall in front of me. A terrible howl escapes my lips. Half-blinded by pain, I look down at my wound, afraid of what I will see.

My chest looks like raw meat. An angry growl echoes in my head as my wolf dies and leaves me forever. He took the brunt of the hit; otherwise, I'd be dead already. A shotgun leaves a hell of a mess.

Lorance has disappeared into thin air. Probably stepped into Velox.

I hear Kaya screaming and the sound of a struggle inside the room. *Hurry to act, worry distracts.* I stagger to my feet and break down the door with my shoulder. I see an open window and hear Kaya screaming from under the bed. I hope she hasn't been hit.

On the other side of the room, Lorance battles the ugliest man I've ever seen. The vampire has twisted the man's neck completely around. I can hear his neck bones grinding, but he won't go down. He fires a short-barreled shotgun back over his shoulder and hits Lorance in the arm. I sink a round into Frankenstein's head, counting on the pre-fragmented bullet not to punch through and hit Lorance.

Frankenstein's head lolls but his arms are still fighting. Another shotgun round goes off, this one into the wall behind Lorance.

Feeling lightheaded, I stumble toward the melee. The room seems to be getting brighter. I twist the shotgun from the hands of the undead man and use the butt to break his knees out from under him. He goes down in a pile, his fingers still blindly clawing at Lorance.

I'm looking up at Lorance now as he hovers over me. How did I end up on the ground? Through my blurry vision, I see his dangling arm pouring blood.

Lorance's voice sounds strained. "Hold on, Stefan. The ambulance is coming."

When did he call an ambulance?

Somewhere in the background, I can hear Kaya mumbling and crying. "He came in through the window."

As my mind wanders to the past, I find myself standing in the midst of the proud Corby Clan, watching as my younger self emerges from my father's house. Young Stefan, prepared for his blót, steps into the night with a shaved head and a fresh wolf tattoo. The kid is supposed to be a great fighter, but he looks too skinny for it. His family follows him, and the crowd behind his family, as he takes the trail out of town and down into the Wolf's Den.

We all crowd into the underground cave, dark rock rippling with rivers of white calcium deposits. Young Stefan kneels on the cylindrical blót stone and looks up through the opening in the ceiling of the cave. Orion, the Hunter, stares down on him from the night sky. The time must be now, while the constellation is perfectly aligned.

I hear the beat of drums as Neil Torp, the Summoner, approaches with a wolfskin draped over his head and body. He whispers something and the boy closes his eyes.

We all feel a tingle as a wolf spirit approaches. To everyone's surprise, the Summoner turns the wolf away. No one has ever seen this happen. Young Stefan, unattuned, doesn't even notice.

Is that how my blót really happened? Why was the wolf rejected? Why didn't my parents tell me?

Moments later another wolf approaches and the Summoner accepts Him.

I remember that feeling as the wolf enters me. It was like being blind my whole life and then suddenly seeing for the first time. It was heart-pounding excitement mixed with gut-wrenching terror, and it would take years to learn how to use this new gift.

I hear Lorance's voice calling me back from the blót. "Stefan, stay awake. They're almost here."

The world has gone from white to black and I can't see Lorance. I suddenly remember the ugly man Lorance was fighting, and I realize why the man was here. It takes enormous energy for me to speak. "Someone else is looking for Emma. You have to find her before they do."

His voice is far away. "That's your job, Stefan. Stay with us."

"Look for her in Newport, Refuge d'Amoureux."

"Look for her yourself. You will survive this."

"Nah, men like me don't die of old age."

I feel strange, tingling and warm. For some reason I hear the voice of the Summoner. "The Trickster is coming."

Who is the Trickster? I have a feeling I'll know soon.

As my life ebbs away, I whisper to Lorance, "Tell Emma..." *Tell her what? That I love her? Do I even know what love is?*

My voice is gone. I can no longer feel my body. This is all too familiar. I've died in battle many times, in many lives. I'm getting used to it now.

Run Like Hell

Emma Rue

By morning I'm exhausted and starving. Cassandra's room is a mess. I spent the night tearing it apart and found nothing. The dagger isn't here. If I want it, I'll have to venture out into the mansion to find it.

Is Julian asleep now, or is he lying in wait for me? Where would he hide the dagger? I think of the places where he spends time, his bedroom and the creepy basement. Do I dare to search these places? What will he do if he discovers me?

I need help with this, but there's no one I can call. Melita has two girls to care for, one of whom is pretty messed up because of me. It must be nice to have a family to help you. I have no one. Not even a boyfriend. Stefan might have become that, but now he hates me. I guess I can't blame him.

I feel an ache in my heart as I realize how alone I am. Tears fill my eyes as I think of how excited I was by the idea of meeting Julian, a powerful man who would love me. I was so…naive. I should have known that girls like me, thrown away by their own mothers, don't get fairy-tale endings.

With my tears threatening to become sobs, I take a tight grip on my emotions. I am *not* alone. I have Cassandra. She is like an older sister to me, and I will not disappoint her by breaking down. I wipe my face and venture out of the room.

I creep toward Julian's bedroom, wincing at every squeak the floor makes. *Please please please don't let him be in there.*

I can see that his door is open. I ease up to it and peek inside. To my great relief, his four-poster bed is empty. I poke my head in and find the whole room unoccupied. I slip inside. What if he is watching somehow? What if he's hiding under the bed, waiting to grab my ankle? My gut clenches and a drop of sweat rolls down my forehead. My feet don't want to step any farther inside. Maybe they're smarter than I am.

My whole body trembles as I ease into the dark bed-chamber. I move over to the windows and pull back torn curtains as thick as an Ottoman rug. Light streams in, revealing the details of Julian's ocean-themed room.

I check the obvious thing first, a hardwood desk with a hand-carved model of an old sailing ship. The drawer is full of old bills from various utility companies. No sign of the dagger.

Where else could he have hidden Síndóm? My wandering eye leaves the closet and settles on the giant chest at the foot of the bed. Did he hide the dagger with Elizabeth's stuffed body? That would be just like him.

I approach the huge chest. I don't know if I have the strength to do this. Even the thought of bodies makes me queasy. At least I don't have any food in my stomach to throw up. My hands shake badly as I slowly reach down and lift the heavy lid.

Elizabeth lies inside, staring at me. I jump back and the lid slams shut. That is wicked creepy. She looks so alive! It feels like she's watching me, like she will somehow tell Julian that I disturbed her rest.

How could he have done this to her? Julian, the great love of Cassandra's life, has somehow taken a turn into evil and madness. Can a lost love really do that to a man, or was Julian's mind broken from the start? Maybe Cassandra was simply blind to his faults. Maybe every vampire thinks her Maker is perfect.

I gather my courage and lift the lid of the chest again. Trying not to look into Elizabeth's eyes, I search around the edges of her body with my trembling hand, finding nothing. What if the dagger is *under* her body? The thought of touching her makes my skin crawl. But I've come this far. I shouldn't give up now.

I lean in and put my arms around her, unsure if I'm strong enough to lift her. But the preserved body is very light. She must be hollow inside, like a chocolate rabbit.

What an appetizing thought. I drop her on the bed, fall to my knees, and dry-heave.

When I finally get control of my stomach, I crawl over to the chest and look inside. My heart sinks as I find it empty. But wait, what if there's something under these velvet cushions that were supporting Elizabeth? What if there's a false bottom?

I tear the cushions from the chest. There's nothing beneath them. I use my arm to measure the depth of the chest, and then compare that to the exterior height of the chest. It doesn't add up. There's definitely a hidden space at the bottom!

I dig around inside until my fingernails find a recess along the bottom. I lift a big plank of satin-covered wood from the bottom of the chest, revealing a hidden compartment.

Inside lie many crumbling stacks of what look like old-fashioned one-hundred-dollar bills, only without any pictures of the presidents. There is also a small wooden box. It seems familiar, like something from Cassandra's memories. It's the box that Síndóm came in! I snatch up the box but it feels too light to be holding the dagger.

The hinges break as I open the box. It's empty. I want to scream my frustration but I don't dare make any noise.

Beneath the box is an old note written on paper that's brown and cracked with age. I carefully open it and squint at the faded ink, written in a graceful hand...

Mr. St. Fleur, it has come to our attention that you have an artifact in your possession that was unlawfully acquired from the previous owner. Below are instructions on how to return it. In the interest of peace, we would appreciate your full cooperation in this matter. If left unresolved, this may attract the attention of the Venatores, an outcome we all wish to avoid.

Faithfully yours,

Hope Fenwick, Speaker for the Town of Newport.

Someone has torn away the bottom of the note, removing the instructions. Who are the Venatores? I never encountered them in Cassandra's memories. I return the note and the box to the chest.

I remember Hope Fenwick from Julian and Cassandra's bloodmate ceremony. She was a member of the Black Rose Society. Why didn't Julian follow her instructions and give the dagger back? Was it because he had already given it to Cassandra? What on earth does this dagger do, and why is it so important to everyone? I have to find it and return it to whoever is tormenting Kaya.

Where to look next? The basement, I suppose. I really hate that place. And what if Julian is there?

The thought of returning Elizabeth to the chest is more than I can bear. Anyway, there's no sense in trying to cover my tracks. Julian would notice if the slightest hair was out of place, and he'll be able to smell that I've been here. I need to finish my search quickly, and then I need to leave this house and run like hell.

The basement smells like death. The stench makes my eyes water. I pull my shirt up over my nose but it barely helps. I hold up a candle, revealing the heaps of disintegrating cardboard boxes and old wooden crates. I doubt that Julian hid the dagger there. It's too important to be stored so casually in the open. He would keep it in a secret place. Perhaps one of the leather-bound trunks?

As I step deeper into the basement, toward the furnace on the far side, I feel Julian's presence. A stab of fear shoots through me. Is he sleeping inside the furnace again? Why would he do that when he has a comfortable bed upstairs? Then again, why does Julian do anything?

I hear a soft noise behind me. Maybe Julian isn't in the furnace—maybe he has come down the stairs behind me! Instinctively, I run away from the sound, plunging ahead. I look up, remembering to watch for the low-hanging pipe I banged my head on once before. My feet catch, and I trip and fall into a pile of something wet and cold.

I recover the dropped candle. By some miracle it is still burning. Its light reveals a horror.

I am sitting on a pile of bloody female bodies. One of them is the long-haired girl from the club, the one I picked for Julian to take home. In her dead eyes I see an accusation that fills me with guilt and shame.

When I turned eighteen, a psychic told me my future. She said in ten years I would be married and a famous writer. She neglected to mention this little horror show. I doubt a thousand psychics could have predicted that I'd soon be sprawled on a pile of bodies in a vampire's lair.

Julian's tired and angry voice echoes from inside the cold furnace. "I'm sleeping. Begone or taste my wrath!"

I leap to my feet and race back toward the stairs, passing a huge rat. That must be what made the noise behind me and sent me running. No doubt it's one of Julian's relatives.

By now, he must have realized that I've discovered the bodies. Will he chase after me? Will he even care?

This terrible game is over. I have to go now. I want to mourn these poor girls but now is not the time. I scramble up the stairs and run for the front door.

But something makes me pause.

Will leaving this place really solve my problem? Or is that just something that I want to believe? I ran away once, and Julian found me. He will find me again. I can run forever, but I will never be free of him.

So what do I do? More bargains with the devil? More compromises? That has only brought disaster. My instincts tell me that Julian will break every promise he makes to me, and one day will kill me. So it's time to listen to my instincts and act on them. I should probably kill him first, but he's far too powerful for me. I need an ally. Someone who can stand up to him. Someone like his Maker. Angelo!

What if I can find a way to free Angelo from the sepulcher? He once loved Cassandra. Would that be enough to make him want to help me? I think back to when I first came here and discovered the crypt behind the mansion. Was that Angelo's presence calling me? Was I feeling his love for me?

What if Angelo is just like Julian? What if he's worse?

On the other hand, do I really have anything to lose at this point?

Daisies on the Ceiling

Cynthia Greene

After my fight with the vampire and the werewolf, I wake up in my own bed and see the painted daisies on the ceiling. I'm home again! I smile at the picture of Bill on my nightstand, always watching me as I sleep.

What about my body? This feels like my original body. Has Rowan returned it to me? But what if she left me horribly disfigured? I race into the bathroom and look in the mirror on the door. It's the regular me, with my beautiful gray eyes and brown hair! I pull off my nightgown and check the rest of my body. I'm completely intact, in better shape now than when I died in prison. Rowan has been merciful, despite my failure!

This time around I will do things differently. I will change my name and move to a place where the police will never find me. Then when everyone has forgotten my face, I will reunite with Bill and we can be together. Of course, I'll have to get rid of the Heifer first.

A strange thought occurs to me. What if this has all been a bad dream? What if I was never arrested and sent to prison? What if I never took my life and became Rowan's servant? Is it possible that *none* of this nightmare actually happened?

After urinating and thoroughly sanitizing my hands, I get dressed and go into the kitchen to make my peppermint tea. My lovely kitchen hasn't changed. Spices and teas arranged alphabetically, everything in its place. I will be sad to leave this house, but it's better than going to prison. It's only a matter of time before the police figure out that I'm alive again.

I hear the doorbell ring. I feel a flutter of fear in my stomach. Something about this moment is strangely familiar. On leaden feet, I walk to the front door and peer out the peephole. It's Lieutenant Powers, the hard-eyed brute who arrested me!

I suddenly realize that this is the *actual day* I lost my freedom, the first day of my torturous descent into hell. Rowan has played the cruelest trick of all, making me believe I was free, that I was past all of this.

My heart pounds and my body shakes. Lt. Powers rings the doorbell a second time. I can't go through this again. I *won't* go through this again.

I run into the bathroom and throw open the medicine cabinet. I alternate between handfuls of water and handfuls of pills, swallowing down every tablet and capsule I have. With any luck, I will die before they can get me to the hospital.

Will Rowan be waiting to capture my soul? If she does, I will beg her forgiveness. I will do better next time.

The pills burn like fire in my stomach.

It takes the police a while before they decide to break down the front door. They are too late now; already the world grows dark. With any luck, this time I can avoid Rowan and be reincarnated into a new body, perhaps a pretty blonde with blue eyes. When I am reborn, I *must* remember who I am and what I want.

My name is Cynthia Greene, and I love Bill Higby.

My name is…Cynthia Greene. I love…Bill Higby.

My name is…Cynthia….

After my fight with the vampire and the werewolf, I wake up in my own bed and see the painted daisies on the ceiling. I'm home again! I smile at the picture of Bill on my nightstand, always watching me as I sleep.

What about my body? This feels like my original body. Has Rowan returned it to me? But what if she left me horribly disfigured? I race into the bathroom and look in the mirror on the door. It's the regular me, with my beautiful gray eyes and brown hair!

I'm suddenly sick with dread, realizing this is the day I was arrested. Rowan is making me relive it again and again, probably for an eternity. Tears flood my eyes. I may have failed her, but no one deserves such a horrible fate.

Open Sarcophagus

EMMA RUE

As I approach the overgrown sepulcher, the midday sun reveals the twin angels guarding the false door. Their faces are different this time. They look…relieved.

I feel something pulling me in. Is Angelo drawing me into a trap? Even dormant, he has a strong, familiar presence.

If not for Julian, Cassandra would have become Angelo's bloodmate. How would that have changed things?

As I walk around to the back of the tomb, I realize I have no way to get up to the roof where the entrance lies. Julian and Cassandra could simply jump, but I have mortal legs.

I search around the back of the estate and find a rusted wheelbarrow overturned in a dead garden. The wheel no longer turns, so I drag the wheelbarrow over to the back wall of the sepulcher. It wobbles as I climb into it. This gown is not built for acrobatics. What if I fall? I imagine Julian coming out of the house and finding me with a broken neck. Would he shed any tears for me?

Swaying precariously, I reach for the edge of the roof and find myself an arm's length short. I wish I was more athletic and could jump the rest of the way.

I notice a chink in the wall just deep enough to slip my toes into. From that foothold, I might be able to reach the roof. But once started, I'd be committed.

I take a deep breath to calm my nerves, slide my toes into the recess, and push myself up with all my strength.

My foot slips free and I drop, but not before grabbing the edge of the roof. I swing a leg up over the edge, badly skinning an elbow in the process. I roll up onto the roof, breathing hard and listening to the blood rush in my ears. I look up at a puffy white cloud shaped like a rose. Beneath me, I feel Angelo pulling me closer.

Trying to ignore the pain of my skinned elbow, I crawl to my feet, body trembling with adrenaline, and confront the circle of mossy pedestals on the leaf-covered roof. I recall them from Cassandra's memories. I can unlock the sepulcher by pressing them down in a "C" pattern.

I sit on the first pedestal and it drops down with a click. I repeat the process with each pedestal in turn. As I reach the last pedestal, I realize I'm approaching a point of no return. What if the crypt opens and Angelo comes flying out, howling for my blood?

I sink my weight onto the last pedestal, praying that I'm not making a stupid mistake.

Nothing happens.

I realize that the pedestal never clicked like the others. I slam down on it hard with my hands and arms, jarring myself to the bone, and the pedestal finally clicks into place.

The stone disk in the center groans as it begins to move. It didn't make that noise when Cassandra watched it open. Something is wrong. The gears are probably rusty after two centuries of neglect.

The disk suddenly seizes up and stops moving, leaving only a narrow, dark gap. Is it wide enough to fit me?

I approach the gap and gingerly lower my foot into it. I can feel the edge of the stairs below. My gut clenches as I squeeze my body down through the gap. I have a sudden fear that the opening will abruptly grind closed, cutting me in half. Or what if it closes after I'm inside, trapping me?

Moments later I find myself crouching on the dark interior stairs. I pause to let my eyes adjust. I can smell death, but not as bad as in the basement of the house. A tiny shaft of sunlight reaches down from the gap above me, lighting the face of Cassandra's statue. She really was a classic beauty.

Gathering my courage, I creep down the stairs and reach the floor of the crypt.

Skeletons and decayed bodies litter the floor. These must be the victims that Julian cast in to keep Angelo alive over the years. What if Angelo mistakes me for food? I call out into the darkness. "Angelo? It's Cassandra. I'm here to free you. Don't hurt me."

As I ease farther inside, I see that Tom and Cassandra's sarcophaguses are sealed. But Julian's stone coffin lies open. Is that where Angelo sleeps? Swallowing my fear, I step slowly toward the open sarcophagus. "Angelo?"

I hold my breath, certain he's about to leap out and grab me.

I ease closer and closer.

I jump as a hand suddenly reaches up and grabs the edge of the sarcophagus. On one finger I see a heartblaze ring. *What?? Julian told me he sold it. Why would he have given it to Angelo?*

Angelo slowly sits up in the sarcophagus. But he has the face of Julian! I look past his face and into his soul. It looks wonderfully familiar. It *is* Julian! The Julian from Cassandra's memories. He looks confused, his face hollow and drawn. I throw my arms around him. He smells…right.

Angelo, that son of a bitch, was using his morphing to look like Julian and to mimic his soul. No wonder he didn't smell right. No wonder he couldn't remember anything about his life with Cassandra.

Julian speaks in a slight British accent, his voice weak. "Cassandra?"

"Yes, Julian. You're free."

He smiles weakly, looking into my face. "What are you called now?"

"Emma."

He nods slowly. "*Emma.* I rather like it."

Already he accepts me for who I am! This is truly the Julian who won Cassandra's heart, the Julian for whom I had lost all hope.

I lean forward to kiss his parched lips. Tears of joy flood my eyes as I feel our souls come together for the first time in two hundred years. Our heartblaze rings leap to life, their jewels dancing with the colors of our love.

BONUSES

Respected Reader,

This is your author, Shay Roberts. You have reached the end of the book. I hope you enjoyed it. As a thank-you for reading it, please go to http://shayroberts.com/vsbonus to get the following free gifts …

- ♥ A Vampire Soul bonus story, *Wildwood*. This story exposes Rowan's mysterious Fae past and details her first dramatic encounter with the powerful dagger that will determine the fate of the world. *An exclusive story available nowhere else!*

- ♥ *Emma's Secret*, another bonus story that uncovers the mind-blowing secret origin of Emma Rue, the heroine of Emma's Saga.

- ♥ You will also receive information about Vampire Rising, the next book in the series. Is Stefan alive, dead, or something in between? Will Angelo have his revenge? And what will happen with Julian? Hint, he has an epic surprise in store for Emma!

Grab these free gifts at:
http://shayroberts.com/vsbonus

Happiness is a good book!

Your personal scribe,
~ Shay ~

ACKNOWLEDGMENTS

This book would not have been possible without these great people. Thank you one and all.

Bob Angell, Duncan Barclay, Ripley Barnes, Allan Batchelder, Emily Bradford, Kyle Boyce, Dr. Ray Cui, Julie Gantz, Sage Kahalnick, Ozgur Kavcar, Séverine Trannoy McAllen, Kathy Knuckles, Leila Roberts, Lyla Roberts, Joy Sillesen, Allison Tarr, G. Wells Taylor, Candice Todd, Katherine Tomlinson, Jenna Tramonti, Kevin Tung, Eleanor Uyyek.

36805564R00168

Made in the USA
Middletown, DE
18 February 2019